and other stories

by paul drexel / galhattan press

This book is a work of fiction. Names, characters, places and incidents are used fictitiously. All rights reserved, including the right to reproduce this book or portions
hereof in any form whatsoever.
Galhattan Press 5 West 31st Street, New York, NY 10001
©Paul Drexel Galhattan Press first trade paperback printing
Printed in the U.S.A. ISBN 0-9640300-8-X

Artwork: Paul Drexel. Design and production:

mango shoes

The Little League field was on the edge of the Hudson River across from the Manhattan skyline. Juan sat in the stands watching his son, Gino, play third base for the Cassolino Heat. Joe Favia stood next to him, yelling expletives at the umpire. Favia's son played shortstop for the opposing team, the Unico Dragons.

In direct line with third base sat the Empire State Building. Straight down the first base line was the World Trade Center. The kids claimed these were the foul poles for the stadium.

Legend was, that in 1972 Frank "Babe" De Mielio hit a ball so hard down the third base line that it was last seen ricocheting off the Empire State Building and into fair territory for a home run. Every year for twenty years "Pupie" Romano, who had played on the same team as the "Babe" and who now sold hot dogs outside the fence of the ballpark, repeated the legend to anybody who would listen.

Juan was jittery watching Gino, who was swaying in his shoes trying to stay loose in case a hot smash came down to him and he had to make a play. Balls hit to third base are the hardest to handle in a baseball game. Most batters are right handers and they have to get completely around on the ball to hit to third. As a result, the ball has more speed and the third baseman less time to react. Juan knew the position because he'd played third base in the Dominican Republic as a child.

The game was in the fourth inning and the Heat had a comfortable three-run lead. Cassolino's was an oil company that delivered fuel for heating furnaces. Business wasn't what it used to be before the advent of gas and electric furnaces, but

mAngO SHOeS

Cassolino's still sponsored a team just as they had in the days of the "Babe."

It was hard for Juan to keep his attention on his son's play. He had a problem with athlete's foot and his wife, Marisol, was treating his shoes with an anti-fungal spray that smelled like mangos. There was no escaping the scent. Every time a soft breeze blew or Juan put his head down, he got a whiff of the fragrance.

A woman sitting in the aisle next to him turned to her husband and said, "Do you smell that, honey? It smells like mangos... how delicious."

She kept pinching her nose and holding it high in the air trying to find the source of the smell. Juan put his feet together and tried to muffle the mango odor emanating from his shoes.

Juan came to the Little League games to find comfort. Two years earlier an arson's fire had killed his five-year-old daughter, Jahaida. His mother, Rosa, was also killed in the blaze. Rosa was found lying atop her granddaughter in the smoldering building, trying to protect the little girl. Eleven other people died in the inferno.

Juan, Marisol and Gino were visiting family in the Bronx on the night of the fire. Juan never forgave himself for not being there for his daughter and mother.

The local newspaper printed a brief story about the tragedy; Juan kept a copy in his wallet. It read:

> Early on Friday morning, April 30, thirteen people were killed in a building fire at Fourteenth and Bloomfield Streets. Arson may have been the cause of the fire, which began around two a.m. Among those killed were seven children and six adults. The tenement building was said to have been a haven for prostitutes and drug dealers. Witnesses on the scene reported seeing a woman

lean out a fourth floor window and drop a child into the arms of a cab driver who lived in the building. The child was saved, suffering only a small cut. The woman, however, lost her balance and fell to her death. Another woman was found inside the building, her body draped over that of a little girl, apparently trying to shield the child from the blaze. Several other people died attempting to leap from the inferno.

The owner of the building was the town's mayor. After a two month investigation, it was confirmed that the cause of the fire was arson. No one was ever indicted for the crime. The case was closed a year later for lack of evidence.

The Dragons stranded two runners in the bottom of the third. Joe Favia was standing on top of the bleacher seat screaming at the ump.

He turned to his son who was running to the dugout, "Get your head in the game." The kid looked at his father and shrugged.

Juan was clapping as the Heat left the field. Gino had made a backhand stab and a perfect throw to first to end the inning. The play was close and had saved a run from scoring. The Heat were waiting at the top of the dugout steps to congratulate Gino for his outstanding play.

"Way to go . . . great play . . . all right!" went the cheers.

Juan's son was a study in concentration. He had the perfect demeanor for a third baseman. He had been close with Jahaida, helping his mother take care of her when he was home. Marisol could always count on her son to do chores around the house and keep a watchful eye over his little sister. He took her death hard. Baseball was one of the few places he found solace.

The Heat fans settled back into their seats. The heart of the lineup was coming to the plate. Gino batted in the number three position. His idol was Bobby Bonilla, the fiery right-fielder of the New York Mets. Bonilla used to play third for the Pittsburgh Pirates, batting in the number three position. He was error prone, so he was converted into an outfielder by the Mets.

Although not a great fielder, Bonilla's play was much steadier in the outfield. His bat was always sound, a .300 hitter with twenty home runs and a hundred RBI's a season. Gino was determined to be the next Bobby Bonilla, except he planned on being an all-star third baseman. Gino, like Bonilla, was Latino and from the New York area; to Gino it was a sign of destiny.

The lead-off hitter ran the count to one and two before slicing a single over the second baseman's head. The hit brought the fans to their feet. The Heat were on their way to another big inning, a chance to build on their three-run lead. The second hitter brought the count to two and two before lining out to the first baseman. The Dragons almost got a double play off the smash; the runner leaving first squeaked back to the bag before the tag.

"Safe," said the umpire.

"Hot dogs," went out a cry from "Pupie" Romano.

"I'll take two," said a woman with her hair pinned up behind her head.

The stage was set for Gino. The boy walked over and picked out a batting helmet and an aluminum bat. He was small, but powerfully built for a twelve year old. He stepped into the cage and dug his cleats into the batter's box. A cloud of dirt rose into the air, straight through the mask of the umpire.

"Achoo," the ump sneezed, sending his mask flying off the back of his head. He scrambled to pick it up and the crowd began to howl. Gino stood there silently and cocked his bat in preparation for the pitch.

The Dragon's pitcher shook off the first signal from the catcher. This was no time for a curveball; he was coming with a fastball right down Broadway. It was strength versus strength. He went into his wind-up, cocking his knee high in the air to get some extra kick in his heater.

Juan leaned forward in his seat as the ball took flight. Time stood still as it moved through the Jersey air toward his son. The catcher had set his target for the outside corner. The pitch was like lightening and grabbed the corner of the plate.

"Strike!" shouted the ump.

"Way to pitch," roared Joe Favia.

Juan's son said nothing. He stepped away from the plate and swung the bat twice. The swings were fluid and level. Juan knew his son's routine and Gino's calm demeanor made him even more nervous.

Along with the newspaper article, Juan kept a picture of his daughter and mother in his wallet. He felt their presence in his back pocket and took a breath.

"Play ball," said the ump.

In the batter's box, Juan's son dug his cleats back into the dirt. The wind drew the cloud of dust away from the ump and spared the crowd any repeat sneezes. The catcher called for another fastball. The kid on first was clapping, calling for Gino to drive him home.

The pitch had the same velocity as the first one. The target, however, was the inside corner and this was a fatal mistake. The next Bobby Bonilla had a bead on the ball and began to swing. The bat met its target just above the label. The ding of the aluminum bat had a sweet ring to Juan's ears.

The crowd was in a frenzy when Gino made contact. The ball flew in the direction of left field and was lost against the backdrop of the Empire State Building. It was hooking foul and Juan was on his feet urging it into fair territory.

"Por favor," he whispered while watching the ball slicing

toward the foul pole. His plea was answered.

It cleared the fence just above the sign advertising Biggie's Clam Bar. The Heat's fans were cheering wildly as Juan's son rounded the bases. The two-run homer gave them a five-run lead. Gino crossed home plate with his eyes fixed straight ahead. He gave his teammates a high five and trotted to the dugout. Juan whispered a thank you to his daughter and mother.

The final score was six to three. The Unico Dragons scored two runs in the fifth inning thanks to the play of Joe Favia's son. It wasn't enough to catch the Heat, but it was enough to fill Favia's ego.

"That's my boy," he said to everybody in the bleachers. Juan met his son by the concession stand and treated him to a hot dog and a cream soda. The boy was ravenous. Across the street from the field they spotted Midnight, who was praying in front of a statue of the Virgin Mary.

In the Latino community it was accepted that Midnight saw religious visions. He was nicknamed for his twelve a.m. vigils at St. Francis' Church, where he would communicate with the Saint from Assisi.

Midnight was the first person at the scene of the fire that killed Rosa and Jahaida. He said he was warned about the inferno by St. Francis. He was too late to save any of the victims, but he did fall to his knees and offer last rites for those caught in the blaze. Juan was always grateful to Midnight for guiding his mother and daughter to the gates of heaven.

The boy's cleats clicked on the sidewalk as they made their way home. They lived only three blocks from their old apartment building which had since been converted into condominiums. The store on the first floor sold Godiva chocolates and stuffed teddy bears. Juan and Gino walked two blocks out of their way to avoid passing the building they used to call home.

mango shoes

"You had a good game," Juan said to his son.

"Thanks, Dad," the boy replied, finishing the last bite of his hot dog.

Juan and his family now lived in a subsidized housing complex. The city provided them with the apartment after the fire. Their rent was controlled at a rate of five hundred dollars a month, all utilities included.

Juan opened the vestibule door and checked the mailbox. There were coupons for everything from a deal on boneless chicken at Waldbaum's, to an offer for life insurance from Prudential. There were two other pieces of mail. Gino was already half way up the steps to their apartment.

Juan turned over one of envelopes to check the return address. It was from the Ortiz Funeral Home. It was their monthly bill of one hundred dollars to pay off the funerals. The cost of the wakes and burials was ten thousand dollars. They still owed seventeen hundred dollars to Ortiz. Juan drove a delivery truck in Newark during the day. He had a second job at night, driving a cab, to meet the extra expense.

When he got up to the apartment he found his son slumped in a living room chair watching the Mets play. Bobby Bonilla was at bat and the boy was studying his every move. Juan sat next to him and began taking his shoes off.

"Hi, boys," Marisol said coming in from the bathroom. She was carrying the can of athlete's foot spray in her hand.

"How was the game?" she asked, handing the can to her husband.

"We won," the boy said.

Juan bent over and aimed the canister into his left shoe. The sweet scent of mangos filled the room as Bobby Bonilla smacked a drive down the right field line. Above the television was a photograph of Rosa and Jahaida taken the year before the fire. Juan stared at the picture as Bonilla slid into third.

"Safe!" yelled his son.

"Safe," Juan echoed as Bonilla called for time to dust his uniform.

Juan aimed the canister into his right shoe. The smell reminded him of his mother picking mangos in the backyard when he was a child in the Dominican Republic. The spray rose in the air in front of the blue light of the television, in front of the photograph of Rosa and Jahaida.

Juan placed the mango-scented shoes beside his chair and slipped back in his seat to watch the rest of the game.

mAngO SHOeS

squish

The fourth bug squishes against the windshield of the truck. They hit the glass with high impact and don't have much chance in this encounter. Snap your fingers and you get the noise they make as they collide with certain death. At an average of four bugs an hour, I figure we'll squish another twelve and one-half bugs before we get to New York.

We are just passing Baltimore. The Oriole's new Memorial Baseball Stadium at Camden Yards marks a corner of the city's skyline. Luke's got his arms resting on the steering wheel as we move up Interstate 95. He's been driving since four thirty a.m., making this an eleven hour day already.

All these bugs hitting the windshield are a sure sign of spring. I'm as horny as an 18 year old—another sure sign that spring has arrived. I can't stop thinking about Lisa Portnoff.

This morning in the dark, on the way down South, we passed a sign on the New Jersey Turnpike that read, "Metuchen Exit 10." I have never been to Metuchen, but that's where Lisa is from and just the thought of her hometown is making me all spring inside. Unrequited love has got me snapping my fingers to the rhythm of the kamikaze bugs.

We hadn't had the radio on all day, so we didn't know the latest news about the recent riots in Los Angeles. Luke and I had just come from Washington, D.C. The city was tense. Baltimore had a similar edge. The two of us were glad to be back out here on the road with the bugs squishing into the windshield.

In Delaware, we stopped for some diesel and I bought the Philadelphia Inquirer. I read it over lunch in Bethesda, Maryland, at a place called Mario's. Luke and I had the same thing, an Italian sub and a Miller Draft beer. I asked the gum-chewing, round-shouldered, stay-out-of-the-sun blonde behind the counter for oil and vinegar on mine.

She put her elbow on the counter and said, "Mayonnaise?" "No," I said, "but could I have a glass for the beer?"

She looked at me like I was crazy.

"What kind of a man leaves the mayonnaise off an Italian sub and asks for a glass to drink a beer?" her eyes said.

After the first bite I discovered she had taken it upon herself to restore my manhood with a thin layer of Hellman's spread across the sandwich. I washed it down with the glass of beer. Luke's sub also had mayonnaise; he didn't much care.

We sat across from each other reading sections of the newspaper. Every once in a while, Luke and I picked up our heads and smacked our lips as we read about Los Angeles.

"The fire next time," Luke said, quoting James Baldwin.

I shook my head and kept reading about the carnage in L.A. A few times, I was distracted by my Spring desires for Lisa Portnoff. My heart and mind were in Los Angeles, but the rest of my anatomy was in Metuchen, New Jersey.

The eighth bug has just smashed into the windshield. We are passing a trailer with eight horses inside. The horses are calm and I ask Luke if they sedate horses for trips.

"Sometimes," he says, "but not if they're racing on the same day."

Luke is fifty-seven years old. I call him the "roadside minister." Working with him is like a baptism — only somebody forgot the water. We joke, sing, we share our views about life. On this trip, we have spent a good bit of time in silence, watching the bugs collide with the truck's windshield.

Up ahead is an old blue bus. Directly behind it is a sheriff's jeep with a sign on the side door that reads, "Maryland State Police." As we pass the bus, we notice it is filled with prisoners who are all black. The two cops in the jeep and the two cops in the bus are white.

Luke gives a prisoner the thumbs up sign. The prisoner raises his arms to reveal a set of shackles. He gives a tired smile and disappears behind us in the exhaust of our truck. Luke looks into the rear view mirror and says:

> Testify! Testify!
> If I never, never see you anymore!
> Testify! Testify!
> I'll meet you on Canaan's shore!

"Where's that from?" I ask.

"Sounds biblical," Luke says.

I decide to turn on the radio to get in touch with the outside world. We are nearing Delaware and the Baltimore station is fading. Between the static, Luke and I listen to the news about the riot in Los Angeles:

> The Los Angeles Fire Department reports that all but two of the 3,767 fires that have raged throughout the city since Wednesday are under control . . . (static) . . . The death toll from the violence stands at 38, surpassing the total of 34 who died during the seven days of the Watts riots in August 1965 . . . (static) . . . 1,419 people are injured and more than 4,000 people are under arrest . . . (static) . . . In Baltimore, Washington, D.C. and New York, businesses are closing early as apocalyptic fears spread throughout the country . . . (static)

I reach over and flick off the radio. The sound of traffic is the only noise in the truck for a couple of minutes. The silence is broken by the eleventh bug snapping into the windshield.

"Next, they'll be calling General Schwarzkopf back from his book tour," Luke says.

A fly has managed to get into the cab of the truck. The fly

is on the dashboard in front of me. It has a good view of the squished insects on the windshield. My first instinct is to swat it, but I figure there are enough bugs dying on this ride.

The road is crowded. To our left is a flatbed truck hauling a giant teepee. The teepee looks at least twenty feet high and is made of plaster. There is a plaster cast guy climbing a ladder alongside the teepee. He has a big sign attached to his back which reads, "Sacca General Contractors, We Repair Anything."

We are crossing the Susquehanna River, near the border between Maryland and Delaware. There is only a small barrier along the edge of the bridge. From my seat, all I can see is the river two hundred feet below. Vertigo begins to set in and I keep reminding myself that Luke's got things under control.

The truck continues to move at a steady pace as we cross the border. A placard proclaims Delaware to be the first of the original thirteen states. As a tribute to this distinction, the thirteenth bug squishes against the windshield.

The bug's impact makes the fly jump and whip around the cab looking for an escape. Finally, it settles down on top of the visor above Luke's seat. Luke pays no attention to the fly. He has one arm draped over the back of his seat while he steers with the other.

"I have to pee," I announce to Luke.

"I'll pull into the next rest stop," Luke says.

Rest stops on the Interstate are the oases of American culture. They are the forefathers of the mall. You can buy everything from microwave popcorn to a lifetime membership in the Knights of Columbus at a rest stop. At some of them, you can even take a shower by putting a quarter in a slot every three minutes to keep the water running.

We pull into the Elsmere Rest Stop, which, according to the sign, is famous for its dairy products. The Interstate cuts through only a small portion of Delaware, so this is the one

squish

rest stop in the state. Luke parks the truck alongside the Elsmere Eat `N' Run. We jump out of the truck, stretch our backs, and head into the establishment.

The place is empty. The men's room is the first door on the left as you enter the building. We both go in to relieve ourselves. I'm the first one finished and I go outside to wait for Luke. There is a black guy watching a television with his feet up on the counter of the information desk in the lobby.

"What's the news from Los Angeles?" I ask.

"There is still a lot of looting going on," he says. "They say the Governor is sending in the National Guard tonight — as many as 5,000 troops. It is a damn shame those cops got away with beating that guy."

"Yeah," I say, "a damn shame."

I tell the guy that we are heading to New York. He confirms the unrest we heard about on the radio. He tells me we should be careful. Luke seems like he is taking forever; finally he comes out of the bathroom.

"Let's go," Luke says.

"Take care of yourself," I say to the guy with his feet up.

"You take care, too," he says.

I get the feeling he means it.

We get back in the truck and on the highway. We are already at the Delaware Memorial Bridge, which goes over the Delaware River. The bridge connects the first state of the union with the third state, New Jersey. The sign welcoming us to New Jersey reads, "Governor Jim Florio Welcomes You to the Garden State."

We have been on the road for almost fifteen hours. Both of us are tired. We fall silent as the New Jersey landscape races by our window. Neither Luke nor I know what to expect when we get to New York. The silence is unnerving.

The fourteenth bug squishes into the windshield. According to my calculations, we are still about an hour from

/19

our destination. The scenery takes on a different complexion as we enter the industrial wasteland of the country's most densely populated state.

I curl up in my seat and start to daydream. I am thinking about a trip I took to Ireland when I was twenty years old. In Ireland, I hitchhiked throughout the country. I got rides from truck drivers and sat in a position similar to the one I am in now watching the landscape.

The daydreams of Ireland are no match for the stench emanating from the chemical and gas plants spewing out toxins along the New Jersey roadside. The scene is bleak and the air makes my stomach curdle. I feel like I am going to vomit.

It is getting dark. The fire-breathing landscape is surreal. There are hundreds of towers with flames shooting out of their stacks. Clouds of smoke blanket the sky. Every once in a while a passenger jet roars through the smog to land at Newark International Airport.

A truck moves past us on the blind side. The air draft causes our cab to sway back and forth. The truck's driver puts the left blinker on and switches into our lane. On the rear doors of eighteen-wheeler are the initials G.O.D.

We pull in close behind the G.O.D. truck to form a mini-convoy. There is a toll booth up ahead. Luke asks me to get some money out of the wallet laying on the seat between us. I reach in and pull out three dollars to cover the fare.

The G.O.D. truck pulls into the tollbooth in front of us. I see its driver reach out to give the woman in the booth some money. He has a beard and long hair and looks like Jesus Christ. I ask Luke if he thinks God has gone into a new father-and-son business.

"God works in mysterious ways," Luke says with a smile.

I feel a little safer having the "roadside minister" to my left and the "roadside savior" leading the way into New York.

The Turnpike extension bridge stretches above Jersey City

and I can see the New York skyline on the horizon. There is a fog covering the city. There are a few lights on in the Empire State Building, a few on in the World Trade Center. I look over my right shoulder to catch a glimpse of the Statue of Liberty. I am unable to see her, except for the flicker of her torch. She is lost in the dense air.

Luke is making good time. I figure we'll get back to the truck yard with one and a half bugs to spare. Jersey City seems abandoned. I ask Luke if he thinks I should turn on the radio to see if things are alright in New York.

"I guess so," he says.

> ... this is National Public Radio. New York City has the feel of a ghost town at this hour. Businesses have closed early throughout the city. Reports indicate that shopkeepers are boarding their windows in preparation for a night of unrest. Mayor Dinkins has called on all residents to stay calm. Fears are running high throughout the Nation as shock waves from the Los Angeles riots continue to spread ...

"I heard enough, turn on some music," Luke says.

"Me too," I say, changing the channel.

I tune in WKCR which is broadcasting a twenty-four-hour birthday celebration for Billie Holiday. The sounds of Lady Day fill the cab as we move along the highway above Jersey City:

> Mama may have,
> Papa may have,
> But God bless the child
> that's got his own ... that's got his own.

The G.O.D. truck is still in front of us as we move off the extension bridge toward the Holland Tunnel. The road is newly paved and flecks of tar are beating up against the belly of the truck. I sit up in my seat and recount the fifteen squished bugs on the windshield. Billie Holiday continues to sing in a stark voice as we near the entrance of the tunnel.

"It is a damn shame those cops got away with beating that guy," Luke says over the music.

"A damn shame," I say in a quiet voice.

We enter the dimly-lit tunnel and the radio turns to static. I reach into my bag and pull out two apples. I give one to Luke and we both start eating as we slip into the darkness beneath the Hudson River.

mAngO SHOeS

another man's shoes

Eddie wiped the shit off his sneaker on the side of the curb.

"I stepped in shit, " he moaned as he scraped the bottom with a popsicle stick. "Damn, these sneakers," he said. "Over one hundred dollars and I have to go dancing in dog shit."

"I hate stepping in shit," Eddie ranted as he dug into the grooves of his high tops.

"You can't find a puddle. You look like a fool rubbin' your foot on the sidewalk. You never get it all off. It slips your mind, but never your nose. And it always happens just before the world's most beautiful woman comes strolling down the block. People say stepping in shit is good luck. Just my kind of luck," he laughed.

Eddie was getting frantic. He bent down and ripped the laces from the left sneaker, the one with the shit on the bottom. Then he reached for his other sneaker and untied its laces.

"Fuck this," he said as he pulled them off his feet.

Standing on the street in his white tube socks, Eddie tied the sneakers together. He looked up at the series of telephone wires. He began spinning the sneakers in a fast circle above his head. He held the clean sneaker in his hand as the other one became a blur against the afternoon sky.

Eddie looked like an Olympic athlete. Keeping his eyes on the telephone wires, he let go of the clean sneaker. The pair took flight. The high-priced basketball shoes were living proof of their claim—to make you run faster and jump higher. Even Michael Jordan couldn't have soared so high.

Eddie was frozen on the sidewalk as he watched the sneakers spin above his head. By this time, a small crowd had begun to form and every man, woman and child was watching the sneakers in flight.

The left sneaker cleared the wires first. The crowd below let out a gasp as if they were watching fireworks. "Oooohhh," they shouted in chorus. The laces caught the wires and the shit-filled sneaker began to loop around the cable.

As the sneakers swayed back and forth across the wires, a teenager in the crowd walked up to Eddie and began patting him on the back. Eddie looked down at the popsicle stick in his hand and threw it into the street. The afternoon crowd began to disperse still murmuring to each other about the crazy guy in the white socks.

"I can't believe I just threw away a pair of hundred dollar Air Jordan's," Eddie said to the kid patting him on the back. "Some telephone repairman who wears a size ten sneaker is going to make off with a brand new pair of high tops."

"Maybe," said the kid, "but shit doesn't bring luck when it's from another man's shoes."

Eddie turned the corner of Ninth and Clinton St. on his tip toes. Duke was sitting where he always sat, outside the corner drugstore that bore his name in sweeping letters.

"What's gotten into you Eddie?" Duke said in the slow, pharmaceutical way he spoke. "Man forgets his keys, even his head, but never his shoes."

"I didn't forget 'em," Eddie grunted. "I just got rid of 'em."

A gang of kids were playing Johnny on the Pony across the street. Six kids were bent over hugging each others' waists, anchored by Wayne, the biggest "Johnny" in the neighborhood. Another six kids hurled themselves on to the back of the human pony. Last in line was Crazy Joe.

Crazy Joe weighed no more than 100 pounds, but his leaping ability and knack for finding the weakest point in the Pony always made the difference. With a howling shriek he ran down the sidewalk. The legs of the kids locked together began to tremble in anticipation of the inevitable. Wayne had the best view of the on-coming maniac. He laughed the laugh of doom as he watched Crazy Joe soar in the air in search of the weakest link.

There it was, Joe Stinson's neck. No matter where he tried to hide his head, Stinson's neck was vulnerable. The weak link in the human chain. Crazy Joe was like an aerial sniper. He struck his target with pin-point precision. Stinson never had a chance.

The pony came tumbling down like a deck of cards. Stinson was on his knees rubbing his neck. Wayne was scratching his head and Crazy Joe was standing triumphantly above the scattered bodies.

Eddie crossed the street in a hurry. The last thing he needed was this group of hoodlums getting on him about tip-toeing through the neighborhood in a pair of socks. He kept close to the parked cars as he hustled down the street. He was still half-a-block from home when Crazy Joe caught sight of him.

Joe darted across the street to meet Eddie and brag about his latest kamikaze attack on the local Johnnies.

"Eddie, wait up," he yelled.

Eddie knew he was spotted and broke into a sprint towards the door of his apartment building.

"Eddie, what the fuck is wrong with you," Crazy Joe shouted.

"I want to talk to you." He darted between an old Buick and a `76 Chevy Nova right into Eddie's path.

"What's up your ass?" Crazy Joe snarled.

"It's what's not on my feet."

Crazy Joe looked down at Eddie's feet. "Where are your rides?" Crazy Joe asked.

"They are over on 5th and Jackson hanging from some telephone wires," Eddie sneered. "Come downtown with me so I can get them?"

"Sure," Crazy Joe said with a look of puzzlement.

They crossed the street and made their way through the remaining bodies of the Johnny On The Pony debacle. Stinson was still on his knees rubbing his neck and Wayne was cutting him up for buckling under Crazy Joe's sniper attack.

The heels in Eddie's socks had worn, but it didn't matter. He was determined to go back downtown and get his sneakers.

Crazy Joe couldn't stop talking. "How come you threw a brand new pair of sneakers away?" Crazy Joe asked with a smirk on his face.

"I stepped in shit," Eddie said.

Crazy Joe was on his side he was laughing so hard.

"At least you didn't step in it with just those tube socks on your feet. Man, that shit would have been oozing between your toes," Crazy Joe said.

"Damn," Eddie said, "all I was trying to do was go home, have a coke and down a few White Castle hamburgers. Instead, I get to roam the streets with the craziest fucker who ever lived."

They made it back to Fifth and Jackson in no time. The sneakers were still swaying on the telephone wire.

"Climb up there and get them for me, Joe," Eddie said.

"What's in it for me?" Joe snapped.

"I'll give you those White Castle burgers waiting for me at home," Eddie shot back. "I'll even heat em' up for you."

"You're on," Crazy Joe answered, already half-way up the telephone pole.

The corner hot dog vendor made his way over to Eddie. "Must be your sneakers up there," he said staring at Eddie's feet. "That boy is going to get killed climbing out on those wires."

The smell of the boiling weenies made Eddie's stomach

dance.

"Give me a dog with sauerkraut and mustard," Eddie said as saliva began to fill up his mouth. "And an orange soda," he added.

Eddie stood there, downing the hot dog, watching Crazy Joe make his way to the top of the pole. The weenie was a gastronomical aphrodisiac and Eddie washed down his bliss with the orange soda. The vendor looked on with delight at another satisfied customer.

A group of kids, toting the latest rapid-fire plastic water pistols from "Toys `R' Us," walked by and spotted Crazy Joe on the telephone pole.

"Hey, that guy must think he's a pigeon," one of them said.

They all pointed and began firing their laser-guided water pistols up at Crazy Joe, trying to shoot him down from his perch. Their high-powered firearms couldn't reach him, but that didn't stop them from trying.

Three East Indian women crossed the corner of Fifth and Jackson on their way home from market. Their saris blew across their bodies in a brisk northeasterly wind. The sneakers were blowing in a similar direction. This would make Crazy Joe's venture onto the wires even more precarious.

"I'm heading out," Crazy Joe announced to the small crowd below.

The scene took on the air of a circus act. Joe tested the cable with his left foot. The tension was sufficient to hold his weight, so Crazy Joe continued.

The vendor barked, "Hot dogs, get your hot dogs . . . hot dogs, get your hot dogs . . . "

Eddie thought that maybe the sneakers weren't worth creating such a spectacle. "Forget about it, this is too dangerous," Eddie called out to Crazy Joe.

At that moment, a strong breeze picked up the Hindu

women's saris. It caught Crazy Joe just as he reached the sneakers. His body swayed frantically to the right and then to the left as he struggled to keep his balance.

"Ohhh," Crazy Joe gulped as he fought the wind.

The children continued to fire their high-tech water pistols up at the moving target. "We got him now," one of them cheered.

Crazy Joe was in a life and death struggle high above his captivated audience.

"Ladies and gentlemen, welcome to the greatest show on earth," the vendor cried.

Eddie hunched his shoulders as he watched Crazy Joe dance on the wire. The women's saris began to settle around their bodies, the wind was calming. Crazy Joe had miraculously survived and was becoming confident. Eddie let out a sigh of relief and the Indian women clapped their hands in approval of Crazy Joe's performance.

"Thank you, thank you," Crazy Joe exclaimed as he bowed his head to the onlookers.

Eddie was in awe of the aerial wizard. With his new-found confidence, Crazy Joe reached for the sneakers. He cradled the laces in his left hand as he raised his right hand high into the air.

It was a wondrous sight. Crazy Joe had the grace of a ballet dancer and the courage of a fool. He lifted the sneakers from the wires and grabbed the left one by its sole.

The transition was astonishing. Crazy Joe looked down at his hand and saw that it was full of dog shit.

"Ah! Shit!" he moaned.

His courage oozed away like the shit between his fingers. It happened so fast, nobody could even recall the moment Crazy Joe slipped.

"Woooow," he yelped. "Oh! No!" Eddie screamed.

As Crazy Joe fell backwards, he managed to latch onto the

wire. It was quite a sight as Crazy Joe hung there for an instant, still holding the sneakers by their laces. He was now in range of the neon water pistol demons and they were firing at will.

When Crazy Joe slipped, everybody below began to scramble out of the way. The only person unable to find cover was the hot dog vendor. This was fortunate for Crazy Joe, but not so fortunate for the vendor.

The hot dog wagon broke Crazy Joe's fall and probably saved his life. He came crashing down through the Sabrett umbrella, right into vats of hot dogs, sauerkraut and onions. The force of his landing sent the weenies splashing on to the sidewalk.

"My hot dogs," bellowed the vendor.

He scrambled on to his knees as he tried to rescue his beloved weenies. Eddie ran over to see if Crazy Joe was still alive.

"Are you alright," he asked, fearing the worst.

"Here are your sneakers," a groggy Crazy Joe responded. "Get me out of this mess," he continued.

The three Hindu women removed their saris from their heads as they came closer to see the damage. The hot dog vendor crawled on all fours trying to save his weenies.

One of the water gunboys walked up to Eddie, patted him on the back and said, "I told you, shit doesn't bring luck from another man's shoes."

mAng0 SH0eS

mAngO SHOeS

jellyfish

When I was eight years old, part of my daily routine was to go to Muser's corner store and buy two jellyfish candies. They were my favorite corner store sweet. They came in a little brown bag and eating them made my tongue red. It took all night to get the red gunk out of my teeth. Then I'd go and get another two and do it all over again. Jellyfish candies were a parent's nightmare and a dentist's delight.

It was in this corner store that I discovered the Vietnam War. On April 18, 1967, when I went to get my ration of jellyfish candies, I was greeted by a picture hanging above the rows of children's delicacies. Inside the frame was a photograph of a man in a uniform and the words, "Louis Muser, Jr., MIA."

I asked the man behind the counter, who I used to think looked like the TV ad character Mr. Clean, why he had hung the picture. He said it was because his son, a helicopter repairman, was "lost in Vietnam."

He said his son, a staff sergeant in charge of repairs for the 191st Assault Unit, had gone on a mission to repair a helicopter. A functional helicopter dropped him at the site of the damaged one - he was to fix the damaged chopper and fly it back to the base. He never returned. Monsoon rains hit the area. There was no trace of him or the helicopter. The military wasn't sure if he was dead or alive, so he became an MIA - Missing In Action.

An MIA, lost in Vietnam - that was a frightening thought to me. I had heard about Vietnam on television. Each night, after dinner, my family sat around a 42 inch, four-legged Magnavox TV to listen to Walter Cronkite give the body

mAngO SHOeS

counts of American, South Vietnamese and Vietcong soldiers. The casualties included some of my brother's friends who had returned from being soldiers in Southeast Asia.

I came from a blue-collar neighborhood. I remember the army and navy recruiters who used to show up on my block looking to enlist guys for Vietnam; eighteen year old guys who were the children of Maxwell House Coffee workers and Bethlehem Steel ship repairmen.

On rainy days, the smell of coffee would lay low across the city. In the morning, fathers and mothers, in blue uniforms with paper hats, streamed out of the tenement buildings on their way to the coffee factory.

At night, you could see the glow from the Bethlehem welding plant on the river piers, where men and women built the giant ships that tugs brought in and out of Hudson harbor.

Their sons were prime candidates for the recruiters in shiny uniforms with tales of great adventures in a place called Vietnam.

Vietnam vets were a different breed. These were guys who used to pick me up and tell me I was going to be a singer some day, but to shut up for now.

There was Clarkie, who told his story one hot July evening while I sat on a stoop and blew spit balls at Keith.

He was on a patrol one night and his platoon had stopped to get some rest. Clarkie was supposed to be the eyes up front. All of a sudden he spotted these "Viet Cong" sneaking up their flank. All Clarkie could do was toss a grenade to stop the guerrillas from getting to the other guys. He said their bodies went off in a million directions, along with his left foot. Only two guys from Clarkie's platoon were killed, and for his heroic act he got the medal he was wearing. He had to leave his foot in Vietnam.

There was also Vinnie, who drove an Opal GT and used to show me his collection of rifles.

"Man, this M-16 is why I'm here talkin' to you," Vinnie would say as he ran his hand along the gun's barrel.

Back then, I was never really sure what he meant, but I figured Vinnie must know what he was talking about. After all, not everybody in the neighborhood had an Opal GT.

Even with these stories and all the pictures on the tube, never did I stop and focus on Vietnam—at least not until I saw that photograph and Mr. Clean told me his son was "lost in Vietnam."

In my house there were mixed feelings about Vietnam. I was listening more and more as my family discussed whether or not my brother should go to Southeast Asia.

In my family, war was an ancestral vocation. My grandfather was a soldier during World War I and my father was a pilot during World War II. My uncles fought for Uncle Sam in the Pacific, and my mother helped build the machines that stopped the Nazis and the Japanese.

None of them were fans of war, they would say, but my brother was studying to be a pilot and he should fight for his country. My brother was learning how to fly out at Tetoboro Airport in the Jersey swamps and now, chances were, he'd be flying over the rice paddies and swamps of Vietnam.

It seemed as if Vietnam was everywhere. When I came home and told my parents about the photograph and asked them what I could do for Mr. Clean, they told me to pray.

For a while, I couldn't go back to the store to get the jellyfish candies because I'd see that picture. After a few days I returned. The photograph was like a magnet and I had to be near it. The rows of candy became an altar, a place to pay homage to Louis Muser, Jr.

Mr. Clean looked like he too was lost and even the jellyfish candies seemed to curl up on their ends. It was so quiet now that Louis, Jr. was in the store. I told the man behind the counter that I was praying for his son. He smiled and said thank you.

They found Louis Muser, Jr.'s body in Vietnam ninety-two days later. The helicopter he was repairing was never found. They recovered his decayed body from a cave, in a remote area north of Saigon. He was identified by childhood bone fractures.

He was called a hero in the newspapers. I often thought about how difficult that year must have been for Mr. Clean and his family. For me, it was a year of awakening to a place called Vietnam.

mAngO SHOeS

goliath and the fire hydrant

In 1965, Dennis Logan began his ten-year tradition of swimming the Hudson River on June 21st, as greeting to the summer. Dennis was a riveter on the skyscrapers in New York. He helped build the skyline that provided a perfect backdrop for wedding pictures and Hollywood movies.

On the afternoon of the 21st, as many as 300 people would show up along the river's edge to give Dennis a three-shot bon voyage. They all toasted Dennis in unison . After the third toast, he walked out to the end of the pier and jumped into the Hudson.

The crowd roared when Dennis made the plunge. On his first attempt, few thought he'd come back alive. Nobody even knew if Dennis could swim. His friends were taking bets on his fate.

That night on the local news there was a report about a guy in the Hudson. The guy was Dennis. He had swam across the river to a pier on 10th Street in the West Village of New York City. The dock there was high and had no ladder, so there was no way for Dennis to climb up to dry land. The Coast Guard was called and they plucked him out of the river.

Events like this made Dennis legendary. He hung out at the Uptown Cafe on the corner of 10th & Willow. The Uptown was a bar filled with Maxwell House Coffee workers, Bethlehem Shipyard workers, Ferguson Propeller workers, iron-workers, and bums.

I shined shoes in the Uptown for four years when I was kid. I watched one time when Dennis picked up Leo and threw him through the front window. This was no small feat. Leo's nickname was Goliath. He stood six feet, five inches and weighed around 240 pounds. Dennis was smaller, but built like a fire hydrant.

They were sitting at the bar drinking cans of Schaefer beer. I had just finished shining Loose Eddie's shoes when I saw Leo sticking his finger in Dennis' chest.

"You got no right to talk about Maggie," Leo was saying.

Maggie was Leo's girlfriend. She worked over at the Blue Point Bar & Grill. She'd always had a thing for Dennis. Whenever the two guys drank together, Dennis would start teasing Leo about how he was going to go over to the Blue Point and stick his hand up Maggie's skirt. He never would have done it, but it sure did get Leo riled.

Dennis was laughing so hard he was choking on his beer. The veins in Leo's forehead were popping out of his skin. Every eye in the bar was on the two hulks as they argued. Leo picked up a cue stick and smacked Dennis across the back. I watched the stick splinter into a million pieces from my hiding place halfway behind the bar. I ducked when a piece of cue stick shrapnel came flying toward my head. When the splinters cleared, I picked my head up to see what was happening.

Dennis was standing in front of Leo and he was still laughing. Leo stood there with a quarter of the cue stick in his hand and a look of bewilderment on his face. The force of the blow would have sent nine out ten guys to the hospital. Dennis was the tenth guy.

"Ha, ha ,ha," Dennis was howling. "That was a damn good pool stick you broke, Leo."

What happened next became part of the Dennis Logan legend. He scooped Leo up and over his left shoulder. Leo was kicking and screaming, trying everything he could to get out of Dennis' grip. There was no escape.

"Put me down, you crazy asshole," Leo was hollering.

"You're gonna learn how to fly," Dennis howled. Dennis

goliath and the fire hydrant

stuck his right arm under Leo's neck and hoisted him over his head. I clutched the end of the bar with both hands. What an amazing sight. The Fire Hydrant had Goliath way above his head.

"Fly, you overgrown behemoth," Dennis roared.

He ran toward the plate glass window near the entrance to the bar. I glanced over at Loose Eddie. His cigarette was dangling from his lower lip. It was his bar and he knew he was about to have an unexpected expense.

"Don't do it, you asshole," was the last thing Leo said before he started flying.

He hit the window with his right shoulder first. The impact shattered the glass. The rest of his huge body followed, crashing through the glass and onto the pavement on Willow Avenue.

Leo's short flight took no more than ten seconds. He landed sprawled on the sidewalk, shards of glass all over the place. Blood ran from a deep gash in his forehead, trickled from a more superficial wound on his left hand. Considering what he had been through, he seemed in pretty good shape.

Everybody in the bar ran through the front door to see the damage. Neighbors poked their heads out their windows, trying to figure out what had caused the big crash. A couple of guys ran over to see if Leo was still alive.

I noticed that there was no sight of Dennis.

"Where's Dennis?" I asked Loose Eddie.

"I don't know," he said looking over his shoulder.

I walked back into the bar to find Dennis. He was sitting back on his stool finishing his beer. He had just hoisted a 240 pound guy over his head and thrown him through a window, and here he was drinking a beer like nothing had happened.

"He all right?" Dennis asked.

"I think so," I said.

"Tell him to come in here and I'll buy him a beer," Dennis

/43

laughed.

I went back outside the bar. Leo was on his feet, shaking pieces of glass out of his clothes. I told him Dennis' offer. He didn't hesitate. It would take more than a couple of cuts for Leo to turn down a beer. He wrapped a towel around his head to stop the bleeding and walked back into the Uptown Cafe.

The rest of the crowd followed. Less than fifteen minutes after Leo's first flying lesson he was back at the bar. The Fire Hydrant and Goliath sat there sharing a beer. Except for the sound of Loose Eddie sweeping up glass out on Willow Avenue and the blood soaked towel around Leo's head, everything was back to normal. Just another day in the legendary life of Dennis Logan.

Dennis kept a horse on a farm out in the swamps of Secaucus. He called the horse "Sugar." On Saturdays he drove at dawn to the farm, groomed Sugar, and then rode him back to Hoboken. Kids lined the road in Secaucus, Union City, Jersey City, Weehawken and Hoboken as Dennis and Sugar made their way to 10th & Willow. The journey took them past St. Anne's Church. This was the church where Dennis' parents had been married and where memorial services had been held for them before they were buried.

Outside the church, Dennis hitched Sugar up to a fence that ran along the side of the rectory. He walked up the steps of the church, took off his cowboy hat, and bowed his head in prayer. It was quite a sight to see Dennis in his cowboy boots on the steps of St. Anne's.

Sugar was a good horse and didn't make a sound while Dennis paid his respects. Afterward, he climbed back on Sugar and continued into town. This was his only stop before the Uptown Cafe. My brother, Rich, and I would cram ourselves out the window of our apartment to get a glimpse of Dennis and Sugar. We lived on the third floor above the Uptown and had the best view of Dennis and Sugar as they

goliath and the fire hydrant

made their way down Willow Avenue.

But horseback riding through the city and giving flying lessons to Goliath were but preludes to subsequent events in Dennis Logan's already legendary life. For on the night of December 7th, 1974, a night that shall live in infamy, Dennis Logan performed a feat that lifted him to mythic proportions.

Pier D caught fire. Watching a pier burn was one of the highlights of life in Hoboken during the 1970's. People would carry lawn chairs to the cliffs by Stevens Institute of Technology to sit and watch the infernos. The burning of Pier D was the most spectacular of them all.

The fire started around eight p.m. It was an unusually warm night for that late in the year. I was hanging out on my stoop with my neighbor, Keith, when two kids came running up the block.

"Pier D is on fire," they kept yelling as they ran by.

The two of us jumped up and ran toward the river. When we crossed Washington Street, we could see the glow of the fire in the distance. We ran across Hudson Street and up through Elysian Park, toward Stevens.

Once atop the cliff we gazed down in awe at the scene on Pier D. It was incredible. The fire had already spread the full length of the wharf. Picture a whole city block on fire and you can imagine the blaze. Flames shot over a hundred feet into the night sky. Fire boats from up and down the river converged on the pier.

You could see people lining the shoreline of New York City. It was Hoboken's big night out. Keith and I were two of the first people to make it up the cliff. By now, word had spread and hundreds of others were arriving for a glimpse of the fire.

The fire had turned the night into day. Its intensity sent a wave of searing heat over the crowd on top of the cliff. Old women were wiping their foreheads with handkerchiefs; old men were moving closer to the cliff's edge to get a better view.

Keith and I had the best view. We were sitting out on a rock near the Stevens cannon, a relic from the 1800's. It had been used to protect the harbor from marauders. Now it pointed directly at Pier D.

"Ready to fire," Keith joked.

He raised his arm above his head as if he was waiting for the signal to fire.

"Fire!" I yelled.

"Fire!" Keith repeated.

We both imitated the sound of an explosion. We stood up on the rock to watch the trajectory of our imaginary cannon ball. Keith and I stood there for what seemed like an eternity. What we saw next was astonishing.

A man emerged from the burning pier with another man on his back. Firemen were standing a few hundred yards back from the blaze. The flames made it impossible for them to get any closer. We watched in awe as the guy tried to carry the other guy off the pier.

He staggered twice. The first time he fell to knees but still managed to keep the other guy from falling from his shoulders. The second time he stumbled forward but somehow was able to keep his balance.

The crowd on the cliff behind us was urging the staggering man on to safety.

"You can make it," someone yelled. "Come on, just a couple of more yards."

The firemen made a corridor for the staggering man with the spray from their hoses. The flames seared the night sky all around the staggering man. He was only a few yards from the firemen when again, he fell. The guy he was carrying slipped off his back and lay face down on the pier.

Flames began to engulf the area where the pair had fallen. Two firemen broke ranks and ran over to drag the men out.

goliath and the fire hydrant

They made it just in time. The fire had spread and the heat was driving the firefighters farther and farther back from the pier. Seconds had made the difference in this life or death struggle.

The two men were put into an ambulance and rushed to St. Mary Hospital. Nobody on the cliff had any idea who the guys were, or whether they had survived. We watched the fire until early in the morning. We sat there silently as the flames died to embers. All that was left of Pier D was smoldering remains. Keith and I made our way home at dawn. Our clothes were filled with the smell of smoke.

When I got back home I stopped into the Uptown Cafe. It was seven a.m. The door was open and there was one guy sitting at the bar. It was Dennis Logan. His head was resting on the bar. His eyes were open.

"You see the fire?" I asked Dennis.

"Yeah, kid, I saw the fire," he said.

His head was still slumped on the bar. He had a glazed look in his eyes. I figured he must have been up all night and was finally getting some rest.

"Take it easy, Dennis," I said and left.

He didn't say a word.

Keith told me later in the afternoon that Dennis was the guy on the pier. It turns out his brother, Lou, was a security guard on Pier D. He was caught in the blaze and lost consciousness. Dennis ran past the firemen and onto the pier to save his brother. In a story in the local newspaper, firemen said they were sure he would never make it off the pier alive. When he emerged with his brother on his back they were amazed.

Lou was in bad shape with burns over most of his body and smoke in his lungs. Dennis suffered from smoke inhalation, but was released from the hospital after two hours. When I saw him at the bar he never let on that he had just run onto the burning pier, carried his brother through the blaze and saved his life. The Fire Hydrant was not only a legend, he was a hero.

Dennis never talked about his heroic act. Except for the lingering smell of smoke, life at the Uptown returned to normal after a couple of days. Dennis asked me to shine his shoes. The shoes' rubber soles were half melted and the leather had burn marks around the laces. When I was finished, I told him it was no charge. It was the least I could do for the guy.

The rest of the winter went by without any incidents. Goliath and the Fire Hydrant sat drinking at the bar almost every night. Lou was making good progress recovering from his injuries. On Friday nights, Dennis brought a bottle of whiskey by the hospital to give his brother a drink.

The blaze was investigated by the fire inspectors and deemed arson. Damages were said to be in the millions. The pier was condemned. Its charred remains sat out on the Hudson for five years. A testament to the fiery end of the Hoboken shipyards.

When spring came, everybody started wondering whether Dennis would swim the Hudson on June 21st. We all thought he had probably seen enough of the piers and the river. We were wrong. On June 18th he stood up on the bar and invited everybody down to Bethlehem Shipyard Pier to celebrate his departure.

June 21st, 1975 was a Saturday. The sky was clear and the temperature was 85 degrees. Loose Eddie called the weather bureau to find out the water temperature that day. It was in the 50's.

"I'm sure glad I ain't the one diving in that cold water," Loose Eddie said to Dennis.

"That ain't water," Goliath laughed. "It's the Hudson."

At least 300 people followed Dennis down to the pier. He

goliath and the fire hydrant

didn't say a word the whole time. When we got to the pier, he slipped his pants off and stood out near the water's edge in his bathing suit.

Maggie was the first one to raise her glass to Dennis. Everybody drank the first toast. The next two were fast and painless. The crowd was cheering in eager anticipation. The three-shot bon voyage was completed. Dennis turned, waved and then dove off the pier.

The last time I saw Dennis he was swimming toward New York City. He disappeared behind a huge barge making its way up the river. He never made it to the other side. The Coast Guard searched for him for three days to no avail. He was lost at sea.

The Coast Guard reported that he must have drowned. They never found his body. At the Uptown Cafe the regulars knew better. Goliath claimed he must have hitched a ride on the side of a cruise ship and was soaking up the sun down in Bermuda. Loose Eddie was sure he'd be back at the bar with a story only Dennis could tell.

Every year on June 21st a crowd gathers down on the pier at the Bethlehem Shipyard to give Dennis Logan the three-shot bon voyage. Loose Eddie rides Sugar down to the pier. Goliath keeps his arm around Maggie for the toast. I stand there with my shot of whiskey toasting the memory of a guy who swims with the fishes.

mAngO SHOeS

caesar is dead/long live caesar

I was getting a cup of coffee in a deli when the woman behind the counter started talking about a fireman who had died. Her eyes were heavy with old tears. She talked in a whisper. I could tell her mind was on things more important than my coffee.

"Can I help you?"

"A coffee on the dark side."

She turned her back to me. Her shoulders were round with sorrow. She began to pour the coffee. A co-worker walked up beside her. She reached for the milk and began talking.

"I've got to go to Caesar's funeral."

"What time does it start?"

"It starts at eleven. They expect over a hundred firemen to come."

"I'll cover for you."

"Thanks."

She turned toward me and put the coffee on the counter. There was too much milk in it for my taste. Usually, I would ask for less, but this time I knew better.

"Anything else?"

"No, that's it."

"Sixty cents."

I put the change on the counter. She picked it up without even noticing me. I wanted her eyes. I wanted to ask her about Caesar. I wanted to know if it was the same Caesar I had known when I was a kid.

"Excuse me."

"Something else?"

"I overheard you talking about Caesar dying."

I finally had her eyes. She looked through me with a gaze that said intrusion.

"Was his name Caesar Morales?"

Her look changed. The red flashing *don't walk* sign had turned yellow.

"Yes. He died two days ago."

"I'm sorry. We were friends when we were kids."

"Caesar had a lot of friends."

"How did he die?"

"AIDS."

The *don't walk* sign was flashing in big red letters. Only this time it was in my eyes. She had said he was a fireman. I thought she was going to tell me he had died in the line of duty. I never thought she was going to say AIDS. I tried to keep my composure.

"Where is the funeral?"

"Elysian Fields."

"I'll pay my respects."

"Thank you."

I began to walk out of the store.

"You forgot your coffee."

"Thanks."

I held the coffee with two hands. I made my way out of the store. The air was cool. I sipped the coffee. It was the hottest coffee I ever drank. Caesar died of AIDS. I couldn't get over it.

I hadn't seen Caesar in fifteen years. We lost touch when I moved out of the old neighborhood. We grew up on the same block. Caesar was one of two brothers. I was one of four brothers. We were rivals. They were Puerto Rican. We were Irish. We all played basketball.

Caesar had all the moves. We called him "Ice." When the

game was on the line the ball always went to Caesar. He would slowly dribble up court and move in on the defender. He'd slip the ball back and forth between his legs. As he got closer to the basket he would stutter-step to the right and then make his move to the left. Caesar froze the defender just long enough, leaving him with nothing but a cool breeze while Caesar glided by for another clutch shot.

Caesar's brother's name was Wolf. He didn't need a nickname. Wolf fit him fine. He was an inside player. He would grab a rebound and growl.

One time some kids from downtown came to our courts to challenge our domain. Wolf was on the prowl.

"Vendjo, I'm going to rough you up," he snapped.

He kept his word.

Across the street from the courts was Papo's Polleria. Puerto Ricans bought their poultry at this neighborhood slaughter house. Rows of chickens in cages lined the walls of the store. There were usually four or five chickens squeezed inside a cage. Chickens are stupid, but even these birds seemed to know their fate.

Papo would stick a bird upside down in a metal garbage can and slit its throat. The chicken's feet would smack the side of the can as it bled to death. It died in rhythm with the Patato Valdez music blaring from the store's radio.

Every Saturday, a fresh bunch of chickens would arrive on the back of a flatbed truck. Their stench would carry across the street and lay over the courts where we were imitating Julius Erving and Nate Archibald.

"I hate those chickens," Caesar would say with his hand across his face. "Chickens and basketball just don't mix."

I decided to take a walk by Columbus Park and visit the courts we used to play on together as kids. Papo's Polleria was gone. It had become a gourmet shop selling fresh cheeses and other delicacies.

mAngO SHOeS

I walked through a hole in a fence onto the courts. I could taste the chicken stench as I made my way to the foul line. The court's lines were faded and the rims were bent. It looked just as it had twenty years earlier.

I could see Caesar standing out by the top of the key orchestrating our team. The memory brought a smile to my face. I was having a hard time believing that the Caesar out there with the ball was the same one who had just died of AIDS.

A kid came through the hole in the fence with a ball in his hands. He looked about thirteen years old. He was dribbling the ball back and forth between his legs.

"Want to play one on one?" he asked.

I had on an overcoat and leather shoes. It didn't matter.

"Sure," I said.

"I'll do or die," he said.

"You sure will," I answered.

We played two games. The kid was quick and had a good shot. I hadn't played in a couple of years, but it all came back. I felt like I was defending the past as we swapped baskets. I beat him both games. The kid gave me a high-five, took his ball and went back through the hole in the fence.

My shirt was hanging out of my pants. I could already feel the ache in my back. My hair was wild. I realized I must have seemed like a maniac to the kid. I gathered myself together and left.

It was eleven o'clock. It would take me at least five minutes to walk over to Elysian Fields. As I got closer to the cemetery I saw nothing but red fire trucks. Hundreds of firemen, in full uniform, were gathering at the gates of the burial ground.

Elysian Fields is an old cemetery. The grave sites there date back as far as the 18th century. Standing at the gates of the cemetery were two guys who seemed out of place. They looked familiar to me.

/54

As I made my way through the firemen, I recognized them. They were the Santora brothers; Mike and Tona.

They were identical twins, but I had always been able to tell them apart. Tona had his collar turned up and was staring at the sky. Mike was wearing a black leather jacket. He spied me as I made my through the crowd.

"How you doing, Mike?"

"I'm all right. It's been a long time, my man."

"Yeah, long time."

"How you doing, Tona?"

Tona never answered. He kept looking at the sky. He was thin. They both were thin. When we were kids, the Santora brothers were the playboys of the neighborhood. They always bought their clothes in New York. Mike even had a pair of leather pants.

One July night, a group of us were sitting on a stoop hoping for anything resembling a breeze. All of a sudden, hell broke loose. Mike and Tona came running out of their apartment building.

"He killed her . . . he killed her . . . he killed her . . ." Tona kept stuttering.

Mike was shaking. He was standing on the edge of the stoop, telling us to call the cops. I'll never forget his face. We got the breeze we were waiting for. The twins' father had come home drunk. He got into a fight with their mother. Domestic violence in a 1970 tenement had its own ring. He shot her with a snubbed nose .44 caliber revolver—twice, in the face.

Death became her. When they carried her out of the building she didn't have a sheet over her head. She worked at Peachy's Beauty Parlor and must have had a perm that afternoon. Every hair was still in place.

Six cops carried her down the steps. I kept thinking about Elizabeth Taylor when she played Cleopatra. She had been poisoned. All of Rome was on hand as they carried her high atop her burial pyre. Cleopatra, Elizabeth Taylor, looked just as fine dead as she did alive.

The twins' mother had the same look. Only their mother could get shot twice in the head and have no blood in her beehive. She was the best looking woman without a face I had ever seen.

We walked along the road through the gates of Elysian Fields. Tona was on my left, Mike on my right.

"What happened to Caesar?" I asked.

"He was a junkie," Mike said. "He stopped usin' and joined the fire department. He got his life together and then he found out he was positive."

"It brought him down hard, but he kept with the job. He even saved this kid's life two years ago. He started gettin' real sick last year."

Tona didn't say a word. He kept staring up at the sky, as if he were trying to get a glimpse of Caesar. I saw the firemen starting to form a corridor outside the cemetery. They stepped to opposite sides of the road. The corridor stretched as far as I could see. A silence spread over the scene. It was time. Caesar was coming.

The procession moved slowly in the distance. Mike and Tona walked to the side of the cemetery gate. For a moment, I was the only one left in the road. Directly in front of me was Caesar's hearse.

I couldn't move. My feet were frozen. The procession drew closer. The hearse was silver and draped in a bed of fresh-cut flowers. Caesar was less than fifty yards in front of me. I tried to move, but my legs did not respond. I was trembling.

I hadn't seen Caesar in twenty years and here I was about to get in the way of his funeral procession. The hearse kept its steady pace. Caesar was nearing the gates of the cemetery. I felt his presence.

caesar is dead/ long live caesar

The crowd began to stir. I saw firemen whispering to each other and pointing in my direction. At that moment, someone grabbed my right elbow and led me to the side of the road. It was the woman who had served me coffee earlier.

She stood next to me without saying a word. The hearse was making its way through the gates of Elysian Fields. A fire truck began to ring a bell. The firemen raised their arms to salute.

This was Caesar's moment. The hearse passed Mike and Tona. Mike blessed himself. Tona continued to stare at the sky. Suddenly, he fell to his knees and broke his silence.

"Caesar is dead, long live Caesar!" Tona cried out.

"Caesar is dead, long live Caesar," he kept repeating as the hearse moved past. His eyes were still on the sky, as if he had seen Caesar's soul pass overhead.

The woman from the deli had hold of my arm when Caesar made his way past us. The glare from the sun beating down on the hearse was blinding. I could hear Tona in the background. The bell continued to ring as the procession glided past.

I noticed a fireman break the ranks outside the gates of the cemetery. He was running along the road and shouting.

"Pier C is on fire," he yelled. Firemen began running in every direction. Fire trucks sounded the alarm as they sped from the scene. In the distance a huge cloud of smoke rose into the air.

Through it all, the woman who had rescued me remained silent. Her eyes were fixed on Caesar. The single bell rang above the sirens of the trucks heading toward the pier.

Amidst the chaos, I spotted Tona. He was still on his knees staring at the sky.

"Caesar is dead, long live Caesar . . . Caesar is dead, long live Caesar . . . ," he kept repeating.

The air was cool. I started thinking about the cup of coffee I had gotten earlier in the morning. It was the hottest coffee I ever drank.

mAngO SHOeS

lemon drops

As I climbed the last flight of stairs, all I could think about was the scratch on the kitchen table. For the life of me, I couldn't figure out how it had gotten there. But, sure enough, there it was, right where my father would put the platter filled with Sunday's roast beef dinner.

When I got to the top of the stairs and saw the apartment number, the idea of living in 3-D brought a smile to my face. The door was ajar, as it always was, and I could hear my mother inside going about the business of getting my younger sister ready for church.

"Hello, Michael," my mother said. "Did you get the paper for your father?"

On Sunday morning, it was my chore to get *The Observer* for my father, who would be waking any minute.

"Sure I did, Mom," I said. "I also got something for you."

I pulled a package of lemon drops from under my coat. These were my mother's favorite and I knew I'd get most of them myself.

"Bought them with my own money," I said.

"As long as it wasn't church money," my mother dryly answered.

My mother and sister were all dressed and ready for the walk to Our Lady of Grace, the Irish church in the neighborhood. My family made their pilgrimage every Sunday to OLG to join in prayer with the other immigrants from the Emerald Isle. For the moment, I had forgotten about the scratch on the table. As I walked over to put *The Observer* where my father would be sitting, I caught sight of it.

To my dismay, the scratch looked as if it grown since the

night before. All of my one hundred and twenty-five pounds sank into my shoes as I spied the gouge in the wood. I pictured my father placing the meat platter and seeing the scratch. I made the Sign of the Cross and slumped into a living room chair.

"Good to see you already praying this Sunday," my mother said.

Startled, I answered, "It's Sunday, Mom, you can never pray enough on Sunday."

"Seems like Sunday School is wearing off on you," my mother said with a gleam in her eye.

The three of us headed out of the apartment. My mother was the last out. She closed the door and hollered to my father, "We're leaving now."

This was a cue for him to get up and have the house to himself. I wasn't so sure if we went to church to get close to God or away from my father. One thing I was sure of was that when he found that scratch on the table I was going to need a new set of knuckles.

The five-block walk to OLG was a quiet one with my sister up ahead skipping over the cracks in the sidewalk. My hand reached inside my pocket for a lemon drop. My mother, with the instincts of a child bearer, shot a glance at me and said, "Not until after church, Michael." I let the lemon drop slip back into my pocket and licked the sugary residue from my fingers.

When we arrived at the church, it was filled with the Irish Catholics from the neighborhood. Italians went to St. Anne's Church downtown. There was a special mass in Spanish at one p.m. Segregation by church doors was an old way of drawing community lines.

At the entrance of the church, I looked up. My sister and mother had already gone through the doors to the family pew. I could not take my eyes from the statues above the entrance way. Each was lined with steel spikes. While only Jesus may have worn a crown of thorns inside Our Lady of

Grace, the whole outside of OLG came equipped with steel spikes. The spikes were in place to protect the church's facade from pigeons and their excrement. I could not help but wonder if Jesus also wore his thorns to guard against pigeon shit.

"Get in here," my mother whispered.

"Oh, hello Mr. Lally," I said as I dabbed myself with holy water and made my way to the family pew.

"You oughta do that twice," whispered Mr. Lally.

Father Dolan always entered the church as if he were a judge. When the altar boy rang his bell, Father Dolan would emerge from the right of the pulpit. His robe was all black. He looked like a Supreme Court justice. The faithful flock stood in judicial awe.

I wondered why it was that we had an Irish priest, while St. Anne's had Father Spinelli. I always thought that a little Spinelli in the church would have made mass a lot more exciting. I could just imagine the Kelly sisters getting their "Irish up" as Spinelli from Spoleto read from the missal.

"Body of Christ," Fr. Dolan bellowed through the church.

"Body of Christ," the faithful retorted.

My eyes were glued on the sixth station of the cross, the one where Jesus gets a hand from Veronica, when an altar boy clanging the vessels of frankincense and myrrh wafted his way past our pew.

When the cloud of ancient odors cleared our aisle, my eyes were in burning tears and I felt anemic. The sixth station of the cross became animated and I felt like I was close to passing out. As I slumped back in the pew my mother firmly whispered, "Sit up."

"Body of Christ," Fr. Dolan bellowed.

"Body of Christ, "the congregation echoed.

Veronica turned toward me and moved her lips. "He is coming," she seemed to be saying.

My eyes were on fire and I felt nauseous. I was sure this was the Second Coming. It was my luck that I would be about to vomit at such a momentous occasion.

"Lamb of God, you take away the sins of the world, happy are those who are called to your supper," Fr. Dolan continued.

The thought of food was enough to make me throw up. I cupped my hand around my mouth just before the eruption. My mother's child-bearing instincts must have been in religious withdrawal. By the time she noticed my predicament, it was too late.

"Blaaa," I gurgled, as I regurgitated into my hand.

It was disgusting, right at the moment of the Second Coming. I managed to glance at Veronica who seemed be turning away, unable to bear the sight of my vomiting. "Forgive me father for I have no control over what I do," I moaned.

The next thing I knew I was on the steps outside the cathedral. When I opened my eyes, there were the statues with the protruding spikes. My little sister was standing above cleaning my hands and face.

"Did I miss him?" I said to her.

"Miss who?" she said as she continued cleaning.

My mother was to my right with Mr. Lally.

"How did I get out here?" I asked.

"You passed out and Mr. Lally carried you out of the church," my mother said.

"He must have gotten sick from the frankincense and myrrh. He always gets queasy from the Lord's incense," my mother said to Mr. Lally.

"He looked like he saw the Second Coming, he was so white," Mr. Lally said as he buttoned his jacket and returned to the mass.

My mother walked over and helped me to my feet. When I got up she took me by the ear.

"Were you stealing lemon drops?" she asked with the

lemon drops

tone of the Spanish Inquisition.

"Nooooo," I squealed as I felt my ear being pierced.

She let go of her grip just before breaking the skin and took my sister's hand.

"We're going home," she announced.

We started walking the five blocks back to our apartment. A half block from the church I looked over my shoulder at its steeple, sure that I had just experienced a revelation.

"Amen," I murmured.

The walk home was on egg shells. My sister kept looking at me with sheer delight. She was well aware of my humiliation and the fate that awaited me back in apartment 3-D. My mother's Irish was up. I could tell by the exacting steps she took along the sidewalk that her pride had been wounded.

Her ears began to quiver, as she imagined the Kelly sisters snickering about my vomiting in church.

"If she fed those children correctly, they would not be so digestively volatile," she heard them gossiping.

Her walk became even more exacting and my fate even more apparent. I tried one last-gasp effort to break the silence.

"Would you like a lemon drop?" I asked my mother.

"Yes," she said. "You should have one too, maybe it will settle your stomach."

I was dumbfounded. By some divine intervention, I had been forgiven for my sins. Here I was sucking on a lemon drop and I hadn't even received Holy Communion. The Lord sure does work in mysterious ways. I was just about to rejoice in the news of my reprieval when I remembered the scratch on the table.

Once again, my weight fell into my shoes. We turned the corner and there was our apartment building. It looked more like a slaughter-house and I was headed for the meat hook. The walk up the three flights of stairs was like climbing a hangman's scaffolding.

My sister entered the apartment first.

"Hi Daddy," she yelled. "Michael threw up in church," she added.

There was no response. The silence was making my head ache. My mother walked into the kitchen and then I heard whispering.

"Michael, come into the kitchen," came the ominous request from my mother.

When I walked into the room, I was overwhelmed by the smell of roast beef. The thought of myself, skewered and cooking over an open fire, seemed like a real possibility. My father was standing in a corner of the room with a piece of sandpaper in his hand. My mother was in front of him, a barrier between me and my ultimate fate.

"Any idea how the table got scratched?" mother asked.

My father's silence was betrayed by the Mount Vesuvius look in his eyes. He was seething and I was his prey. I looked around the room for a savior, but none was to be found.

"Yes," I meekly answered.

The room was shaking, as the human earthquake began to erupt. My mother gripped the side of the table as if to keep her balance.

"Let him explain," my mother tried to arbitrate, but she was no match against the rising tide of male discipline. All bets were off and I knew that I was about to get a whipping.

I raced out of the room. In my heart, I knew there was no place to run, no place to hide. Railroad apartments are built specifically so that raging fathers can apprehend mischievous children without much effort. Life in apartment 3-D was no longer multi-dimensional. It was starkly real as I watched my father unnotch his belt and make his way to our moment of male bonding.

As I ran through the rooms of the apartment, I saw my

lemon drops

world pass before my eyes. There was the picture of our happy family in Palisades Amusement Park. The theme song from the summer resort began to fill my mind.

"Palisades Amusement Park swings all day and after dark . . . ride the coaster, get cool in the waves in the pool . . you'll have fun, so come on over . . . "

"Ha," I laughed.

Here I was about to be scarred for life and I was thinking about the theme song from some cheap, New Jersey, hot weather hideaway. My father heard the laugh. He couldn't have understood the irony.

I made it as far my bed, which was in the far end of the apartment. I grabbed a pillow and wrapped my legs around it. I looked up from my fetal position in the corner of the bed to see my sister and mother peeking into the room, as my father loomed above me with his well-worn-two-inch-wide-cow-hide-leather-belt in his hand.

"But . . . but . . . I . . . ," I tried to explain. It was no use.

"You think it's funny," father roared. "I told you a million times not to use that table for cutting things. This hurts me as much it hurts you," came the inevitable line of absolution.

"Honey," my mother tried one last time to intervene on my behalf, "it's Sunday."

She knew that it would take an act of faith to keep my father from carrying out his responsibility. I made the Sign of the Cross as I cowered in the corner, hoping to add to the religious guilt factor.

He hesitated, but only for a second. God had a mighty hand in our Irish household, but not mighty enough to dissuade him from his responsibility. He was the Lord of this dwelling.

He did not strip my butt clear for a good ol' fashion spanking. I got the ol' catholic ruler-like whack across my knuckles.

"Put your hands out," my father ordered.

mAngO SHOeS

Since they were already in the prayer position in front of my face, there was no hiding them from his wrath. There is nothing in the world like the feeling of a strap snapping against flesh. The belt moves in slow motion and the crack against the skin is excruciating.

"Owww," I cried out as I endured the first whip. "Owwww," I cried out again at the second smack. I watched my father recoil for the third and final blow. "Owwww," I cried one last time and the tears began to flow down my face.

I nestled my right hand in the left one. I watched them begin to swell. The skin was bright pink and for a moment I thought about the sunburn I had gotten at Palisades Amusement Park the last time we visited that crummy oasis.

My father had turned his back to me and was busy putting his belt, my whip, around his waist.

"It hurt me as much as it hurt you," he repeated as he pulled the buckle three notches.

"Palisades Amusement Park swings all day and after dark . . . ride the coaster, get cool in the waves in the pool . . . you'll have fun, so come on over . . . ," I sang out loud, while trying, with my swollen hands, to pull a lemon drop from out of my pocket.

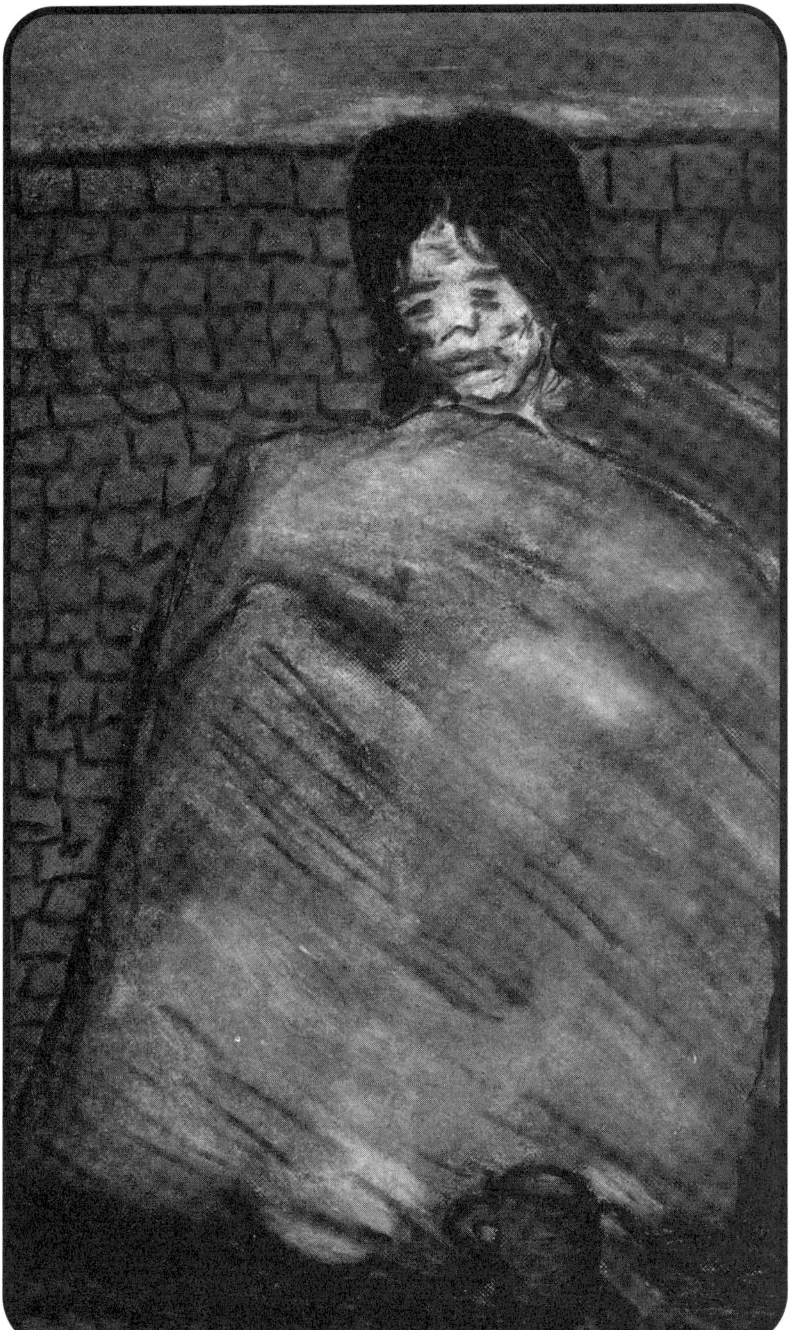

mAngO SHOeS

the electric wind

These were the days of the electric wind. The hour of gargantuan consumption had arrived. The forbidden scent of memory still lingered in the air unrecognized. Jim had already traveled to nowhere a thousand times. His was a tired soul banished to the realm of humanity.

A caravan of velvet cars traversed the road behind the encampment of those unable to make a buck. A group of gray-haired unables pressed their noses against the concertina wire which sealed their fate. They watched the automobiles make their way up the Palisades.

Jim had managed to elude the encampment. His fate was still his own and the scent of memory permeated his nostrils. Bold and colorful men passed Jim on the sidewalk on their way to the base of the Palisades. Jim fell in step behind the bold and colorful men. They provided him with the critical mass necessary to slip by the guards, who bowed their heads into troughs of milk and honey.

At the base of the cliffs, Jim watched the velvet cars make the long climb to the summit. Without the cover of original sin, Jim was vulnerable. He kept his eyes on the automobiles as they made a steady ascent. He began to think of the distant past. The scent of memory swept through the city.

The bold and colorful men had entered a glass enclosure to gorge on a feast of self-delusion. Despite the sweeping wind of memory and the absence of original sin, Jim felt safe as long as the guards continued drinking.

A Roman gladiator, recalled from the assembly line of 400 B.C., rode by on a velvet horse dragging behind him a group of unables destined for the encampment of those with memories. Jim slipped his head into an auxiliary trough to escape the gladiator's eye. When the threat had passed, he lifted his head and licked his lips.

By now, the velvet cars had reached the Palisades and the winds of memory had stilled. It was nearing the hour of forgetfulness and Jim knew he had to find cover. As the guards reached for towels and wiped their faces, a swarm of bees descended onto their heads to feed off the remaining honey.

Jim saw this as an opportunity and leaped onto a velvet horse. He raced past the feeding ground of the bold and colorful men toward the only remaining sanctuary, the town of Arxan.

Along the shoreline south of the Palisades, Arxan had escaped the hour of gargantuan consumption. There, in the village, the electric wind did not blow and the scent of memory filled the air. It was here, and only here, that those with memories could find haven from the hour of forgetfulness.

Jim spurred the horse forward to a necessary pace. Programmed to deliver, the velvet equine could be depended upon to get Jim to Arxan before the hour of omission. With his feet in the stirrups, and secure in the knowledge of safe arrival in Arxan, Jim leaned back and began surveying the landscape of the past.

In the old days, Jim had been a scat singer. As he began daydreaming, phrases emerged from his reminiscent mouth, "Be-bop-boom-bey . . . baba-doo-bop-boom-bey . . . be-bop-boom-bey . . . salum-bo-bey . . . ," Jim scatted.

The music carried him on the hundred mile journey. Upon his arrival in the town, Jim was refreshed in the rhythms of jazz. The journey had been a time for contemplation, a time for memories. He had thought mostly about Ingrid. She was a beauty unlike any Jim had ever seen.

They met one night in a music club in New City. Ingrid had spoken of her work as a maker of wearable art and of her desires. Jim spoke very little. Ingrid's sensuous voice con-

the electric wind

sumed his mind and body.

As he dismounted from the velvet horse, Jim saw the cloud of forgetfulness fall on the Palisades. His were the last memories to return to Arxan. His were the memories of Ingrid.

At the entrance to the town sat a woman selling the gift of life in the form of a bracelet.

"You wear this bracelet and all of life's wonders will slip into your hand," she said.

Her eyes were aluminum gray. The sound of her words revealed nothing but truth. Jim gave her cash for the bracelet, placed it on his wrist, and headed into town.

The town was filled with velvet equine and had the air of a flea market. An artist accosted Jim and asked if he would like to sit for a portrait.

"As long as it is not my own," Jim answered.

The artist became confused and began chewing on the edge of his charcoal, turning his face into a coal miner's nightmare.

Jim thought that perhaps Ingrid had made it to Arxan. The chance that her memories of him might still be alive brought a smatter of scat to his lips. Her image filled his body as he crossed the square, where goats stood on top of circular chairs bloating their stomachs as gypsies played silver trumpets.

Mecca in the town of Arxan was an old Fabian Theater. Here, once a week, as the hour of forgetfulness fell on the rest of the world, those with memories would gather. The people would sit and watch eight millimeter films made before the days of the electric wind.

Jim entered the theater, bought some bon-bons and took a seat among the viewers. The film was called *Roadside Eulogy*.

It depicted the trials and tribulations of animals that had been run over by automobiles. It was graphic, with a cameo appearance by Arxan's former Mayor, Tom Vezzcenti.

Vezzcenti played the leader of a clean-up crew. In the film, he spots a cat that has met a particularly gruesome fate at the hands of a eighteen-wheeler. Vezzcenti reaches down and cuts off the animal's tail.

He turns, looks directly into the camera and says, "This is for good luck." He then addresses the cat carcass, "I'll be back."

At this, the audience let out a collective howl. In unison they slapped their knees and shouted out, "I'll be back." The long-dead Mayor's phrase, "I'll be back," had become the battle cry of those who still possessed memories.

At the end of the film, a public service announcement exalted the need for an uprising against the electric wind. Jim was startled by the face that appeared on the screen. It was Ingrid's.

Jim leapt from his seat and called out her name. The sudden movement caused a panic among those in attendance. Arms flew in every direction, chaos ensued. Ingrid's face was still on the screen as those with memories stampeded for the cinema exit.

Jim flipped the last bon-bon into his mouth as he scrambled through the masses toward the projection booth. In the room, a man was rewinding *Roadside Eulogy*.

The site of animals being run over in reverse was captivating. Jim stood there for a minute and watched the auto-animal carnage. When the reel was finished, Jim gnashed his canines and approached the projectionist.

"Excuse me," he said as he licked his lips. The man turned slowly and caught site of Jim.

"Do you see them down there stampeding over each other?" the man inquired.

"Yes," Jim answered as he looked through the small hole in the wall.

"They come in here once a week and make a mess," he

the electric wind

lamented. "It will take me all day to clean up."

"I'll give you a hand," Jim offered.

Jim and the projectionist made their way downstairs. While cleaning up the remnants of the *Roadside Eulogy* rampage, Jim struck up a conversation with the projectionist.

"Do you know the woman in the public service announcement at end of the tape?" Jim asked.

"Sure," the projectionist answered. "We hired her to make that announcement. The people demand that we have a call for an uprising against the electric wind. They are much too comfortable to take the initiative, but it placates their collective conscience to have a trailer at the end of each film extolling the virtue of overthrowing the electric wind. We have all grown too complacent here in Arxan."

"Do you know where she is staying?" Jim asked, as jazz rhythms began to flow off his lips.

"At the edge of town. She sells bracelets that reveal all of life's wonders," said the projectionist.

Jim was in a jazz frenzy. He looked at the bracelet on his arm. More than scatting, he was stuttering.

"But . . . but . . . I bought this bracelet from her on the way into town," Jim said, showing him the wiry ornament on his wrist.

"Yeah," said the projectionist. "That's her work."

"But . . . but . . . she looks nothing like the woman on the screen."

"That's true," the projectionist said. "Still, that is the same person."

Jim threw the fiber optic broom he was using on to the floor.

"I've got to go," he said as he ran by the projectionist and out the door of the cinema.

The market outside the Fabian Theater was bustling. A young woman stood in the middle of the street defending the

/73

rights of animals in protest of the *Roadside Eulogy* film.

Jim made his way through the masses and past the velvet equine that continued to stride along the streets. When he got to the edge of town, he ran through the gates of the town. Sitting in the same place as she had been earlier, was the woman selling bracelets.

She looked nothing like Ingrid and Jim was confused. There was a large crowd flowing in and out of the town now that the hour of forgetfulness had subsided. Jim walked back and forth in front of the woman, in front of Ingrid.

He studied her aluminum gray eyes, looking for her identity. There was no trace of the woman he knew back in the days before the electric wind.

"Excuse me," he said.

"Yes?" the woman answered.

"Do you remember selling me this bracelet earlier today?" Jim asked.

"Of course," the woman answered. "On your arm you wear the key to all of life's wonders."

"Do you remember me from the days of the distant past?" Jim asked.

"Of course," the woman answered. "You are Jim the scat singer from New City."

"And you are Ingrid?" Jim asked still puzzled by her appearance.

"I am Ingrid," the woman answered.

Jim fell to his knees in front of the woman. "Ingrid," he said. "You are Ingrid, yet you look nothing like Ingrid."

"That was a long time ago," she answered. "Take hold of the bracelet and you will understand the passing of time."

Jim took the bracelet into his left hand. A series of visions raced across his mind. They were visions of Ingrid. They began with Jim and Ingrid seated in a jazz club in New City before the days of gargantuan consumption. They moved

the electric wind

quickly to a time he spent with Ingrid at an amusement park, when he won her a turtle refrigerator magnet.

Suddenly, the images became blurred and the vision distorted. Jim was sure that he was seeing the onset of the electric wind. The sight of bold and colorful men made him shudder instinctively. He clasped his hand over his eyes as he saw vast encampments where gray-haired unables ran their hands along the concertina wire which sealed their fate.

Inside these images he lost sight of Ingrid. He searched everywhere for her. He came upon a field of flowers. The bulbs stretched as far as the eye could see.

Lying in the middle of the field was Ingrid. A herd of velvet equine ran across the field, in front of his path.

The flowers were blown from their stems by the force of the stampeding horses and soon the field was like a dust bowl. Ingrid was alone and her face was fading.

Jim was forgetting what she looked like before the onslaught of the electric wind. Suddenly, Ingrid was gone and the wind picked Jim up and began swirling him in the air.

"Ingrid," Jim yelled.

"I am here," Ingrid answered. "Open your eyes."

Jim opened his eyes. There in front of him stood Ingrid. She was the same Ingrid he had known back when he was a scat singer. She was the same Ingrid he had seen on the screen, calling for an uprising against the electric wind.

Jim put his arms around Ingrid.

"What is it you want?" Ingrid said. "Just say what you want."

"You, I want you," Jim said.

"You already have me," Ingrid said.

"But, sometimes I don't recognize you," Jim answered.

"I am always with you," Ingrid said.

"Even when I can't recognize you?" Jim asked.

"Even when you can't recognize me," she said.

"Do you hear the music?" Ingrid asked.

In the distance, where goats stood on circular chairs bloating their stomachs, gypsies continued to play on silver trumpets.

"Yes," Jim answered.

"I love the sound of silver trumpets," Ingrid said.

mAngO SHOeS

this american day

It is Thanksgiving morning, 1993. At seven a.m. I find myself at Astor Place in New York City injecting the dawn of this American day. The black cube of a white sculptor sits across the street, absorbing whatever light is left from the sunless morning.

Only the forgotten are stirring at this godless hour. The whirring of an exhaust fan, already pumping out the odors of eggs and home fries, accompanies the heralding of a man in conversation with the black cube.

"I'm from North Carolina. Asheville, North Carolina," the man proclaims.

The cube does not answer.

He begins to circle the colorless void. Life in the ten, nine, eight, countdown of the 20th century. The remnants of a man faceless to faceless with a piece of modern art.

"Where are you from?" he haltingly asks.

The cube does not answer.

"I'm from North Carolina. Asheville, North Carolina," the man repeats.

There is no response from the cube.

"I come all the way from North Carolina . . . North Carolina . . . North Carolina . . . ," he keeps repeating.

He walks around the cube one last time. Without turning back, he shuffles into the vacant morning humming "The Battle Hymn of the Republic."

I feel as if it is my turn. I approach the cube from the other side. Memories of the black confessional box of a Catholic childhood emerge as I stand beside the cube. Instinctively, I fall to my knees.

"Bless me, black cube, for it has been and will continue to be since my last confession," I confess.

The cube is still.

Only the whirring fan answers.

I remember my father bringing me to the cube as a child. He hoisted his shoulder against the steel geometric and said, "watch." With the eyes of an eight-year old, I watched as my father hurled his weight against the cube. Legs pumping, shoulder pressing, it began to move. Squeaks echoed across the square. Modern art was talking, my father's legs were pumping, and I was watching through the eyes of an eight-year old.

Remembering this Herculean act, I rise from knees to confront the silent cube. In the name of all the Thanksgiving wanderers from Asheville, North Carolina, I press my shoulder against the cube. I am my father, 25 years later, with the eyes of an eight-year old and the shoulders of a man.

To the rhythm of the whirring exhaust fan, I pump my legs. The struggle is cold and gray. The cube does not budge. I look for leverage and press my weight against the immovable object.

"Answer me in the squeaks of twenty years ago," I yell.

"Can I help you?" someone murmurs from over my left shoulder.

I turn to see my discoverer, only to find that there is no one in sight.

"Is that you father?" I ask.

"No, it's me Officer Reilly," comes the response.

From around the far end of the cube, twirling his billy club in his left hand, Reilly walks.

"Happy Thanksgiving, anything I can do for you?" Reilly says.

"Yes," I say. "Stand there with the eyes of an eight-year old as I get this cube to move," I say.

this american day

"To move?" Reilly says, "Why this thing hasn't moved in twenty years."

"Exactly," I say, "and it's about time."

I slam my shoulder into the side of the metal behemoth. I feel the veins bulging in my forehead.

"Move, you fucking piece of immovable shit," I gasp.

Suddenly, a squeak echoes across the square. Twenty years of sweat pour down my face. Squeak, squeak. The cube starts moving faster and faster.

"Jesus Christ," Officer Reilly says, "that thing does move."

I fall to the base of the sculpture. Its rotation begins to slow and it gradually comes to a halt. I lay there watching the cube: light years of time and space generate from the triangle in the square.

*

Rows of fresh baked bread line the stove. Jean is moving around the kitchen like a Thanksgiving veteran. Her left hand close to her side, she bites on a match. Its sulphur head stands over a pearl onion about to go under the knife.

"I've been biting on matches for twenty years," Jean manages in a clear voice. "It helps keep the tears from flowing."

The cockroaches of the tenement kitchen are nowhere in sight. This is Thanksgiving and they know they are unwelcome. Sweet corn sits in a bag waiting to be husked. Three jugs of apple cider are on the fire escape chilling in the November cold. Jean is still busy biting on matches and dicing onions.

Fourteen people are coming to the feast. In the living room, the Macy's Day Parade floats by on an old Magnavox television. Five people in turkey costumes are controlling the mooring lines of Olive Oil as she glides past 34th Street in Manhattan.

This is the same Manhattan where I was this morning—

on my knees talking to a black cube. Olive Oil is floating by some twenty blocks from the scene of my morning encounter.

I can't help but think that Olive Oil was originally from Asheville, North Carolina. I draw comfort knowing she understands all the Thanksgiving wanderers roaming below her on the misbegotten streets of the "Big Apple." She is the queen of the Thanksgiving Day Parade, the goddess of the forgotten souls of the black cube.

The apartment is beginning to fill with guests for the turkey feast. Ralph and Hilda are busy adjusting each other's clothing as they sit on the couch. Hilda reaches for the American flag pinned to Ralph's lapel. The pin is loose and has turned upside down.

"Ralph, fix your pin," Hilda says in a whisper.

Ralph sheepishly spins the pin back to the patriot position. They both sigh with relief.

Hilda is a German refugee. Rumor has it that she came to the U.S. after World War II. Her past is never a topic of conversation. Ralph was a U.S. Customs Agent and met her just as she was getting off a ship from Europe. They were married soon after her arrival and have been sharing Thanksgiving with Jean for the last twenty years.

They are always the first to arrive for the holiday gathering, and the first to leave. For Hilda, the war is never far away. Her eyes dart back to Ralph's lapel, where the American flag continues to fly high. Secure in a veil of Americanism, Hilda fixes on the Magnavox television. Her past, her present, remain hidden from everyone but herself.

It is my responsibility to furnish guests with a drink. Mary and Ernie, Jean's cousins, are standing next to me and the bottles of liquor.

"Would you like a drink, Mary?" I ask.

"Why, thank you," she responds.

"I'll have a Tom Collins and Ernie will have the same,"

this american day

Mary says.

Mary always speaks for Ernie. She has been doing this as long as Hilda has been fixing Ralph's lapel.

"How have the two of you been?" I ask.

"I have been fine, but Ernie had triple bypass surgery this past year," Mary says. "He is feeling much better," she continues.

"Thank God," I say.

"Thank God," Mary repeats.

I hand the two of them their drinks. Ernie nods, makes the Sign of The Cross, and sips on his Tom Collins.

The party is now in full swing. The guest that everyone has been waiting for, the turkey, will arrive shortly. The table is set. Jean is still busy in the kitchen, taking the bread off the stove and finishing the stuffing. A row of pies sit on a table, ready for dessert. Fourteen carnivores are stirring on this American day.

I begin to think about the black cube. I decide to take a walk. I announce that there is no more ice and volunteer to go to the only open store in the neighborhood. I am greeted by smiles and a request from Jean for a pack of cigarettes.

"I could use a pack of Kents," Jean mumbles, still chewing on a match.

"Okay," I say. I slip my coat on and make my way toward the door.

"Don't be long, honey," Jean says with a faint smile.

"I won't," I reply.

Once outside the door, I hurry down three flights of stairs and onto the street. There is not a soul in sight. I pass a series of windows where families are gathering around their dining tables. I feel the presence of the black cube. I begin to hear "The Battle Hymn of the Republic" and my feet move quickly.

I arrive at the store in a few minutes. As I open the door the guy behind the counter says, "Can I help you?"

mAngO SHOeS

I am startled by his request because the sounds of the "Hymn" are still swimming in my ears.

"Sure," I say. "Can I have a bag of ice and a pack of Kent cigarettes?"

As I make my request I look down at the counter next to the cash register. Staring up at me is a set of Popeye stickers. Right in the middle of the series is a sleekly dressed Olive Oil. She looks cramped and suffocated under the counter glass and in the plastic wrap of the package.

I decide to rescue her. I buy the pack.

With the ice, the Kent cigarettes and Olive Oil I head back to the Thanksgiving feast.

*

I make it back to the vestibule of Jean's building. The room is filled with decorative paint and wall sculptures. Right above the mailboxes and bells is a wall relief of a nymph. Her hands are clinging to a shroud, forever bearing her soul to people getting their mail.

Vestibules are purgatory, gateways between a home and the outside world. They are temporal havens, where city children create imaginary lives and drug addicts live real deaths.

I slump in the corner of the vestibule and dream about past Thanksgivings. I remember when I used to go with my father down to the Macy's factory on the night before Thanksgiving and the big parade.

At midnight workers would roll the floats down to the entrance of the Lincoln Tunnel. There would be elephants and lions from the Ringling Brothers Circus also waiting to journey through the tunnel. They too were part of the caravan sliding beneath the river the night before the big feast. I would stand there, holding my father's hand, as the turkey floats, elephants and giant balloons disappeared into the tube under the Hudson.

I reach into my pocket, pull out the Olive Oil sticker and press it on my jacket. Slumped in the corner, I notice the vestibule's dimensions. It is a perfect square. The walls are ten feet apart and the room has a ten foot ceiling. These are also the dimensions of the black cube. The vestibule is the black cube. I have entered the colorless void. Light years of time and space are generating from the square within the square.

I remember what Jean said about biting on matches and begin to look for one to help keep the tears from flowing.

Right at this moment of Thanksgiving bliss, a car alarm goes off outside the vestibule. I get on my feet to find out what all the commotion is about. Two guys are breaking into Ralph's car. I hear a door slam in the hallway and footsteps rumbling down the stairs. Hilda rips open the hallway door. She has a drumstick in her right hand and a look of rage in her eyes.

"Dey arrr vreeaking into da carrr!" she screams, while waving the drumstick in my face.

We both run out on to the street. The two guys spot Hilda and try to make a run for it.

"Tieves, stop, tieves," Hilda cries out in her German English.

She reaches one of the guys and starts to smack him over the head with the drumstick. He is standing with his hands over his head fending off her turkey blows. She keeps pounding the drumstick down on to his head.

Hilda is impressive. She's got everything under control. One guy escaped, but the other guy is in trouble. She has him pinned with her left foot against the right front tire.

"Quit hittin' me with the turkey," the guy gasps under her attack.

"Verr arr your manners robbing mein car on Danksgiving day," Hilda says.

"Get off me, lady," the guy squeals. "You're crazy."

mAngO SHOeS

He manages to get out from underneath Hilda's shoe. He takes off down the block rubbing his head.

"Dis neborehood ist no good anymore," Hilda growls.

I put my arm around Hilda to calm her down. Ralph comes running over to the car out of breath. He has his Customs Agent badge pinned next to the American flag pin.

"I put my badge on to let him know who they were messing with," Ralph huffs and puffs.

"Come on my Ralph," Hilda says. "Vee arr leafing,"

In the melee Ralph's lapel has turned up. Hilda reaches over and fixes it. Without saying another word, they get into their car and drive away; the first to come and the first to leave. I stand by the curb and watch their exhaust disappear into the dusk of this American Day.

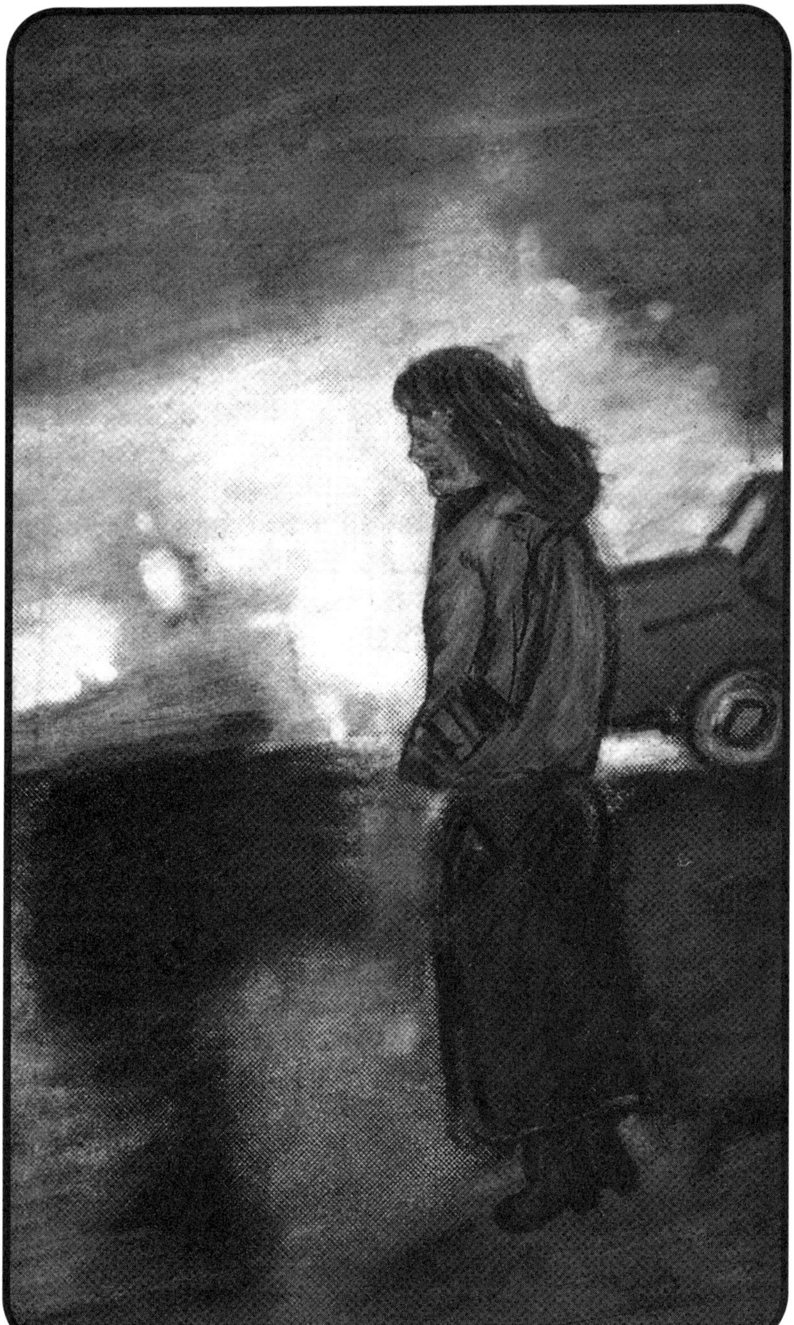

mAngO SHOeS

lefty

Richie did everything with his left hand. He lived three doors down from a Pentecostal church. On Saturday nights he'd get together for a poker game, always with the same two players. There would be no need for a radio. The sounds of souls being saved and visions being seen were enough background ambiance for a card game.

When a lefty deals, the cards move around the circle counter-clockwise. Richie's deal was quick. He thumped every card, so it made a snap as it shuffled to the table. He kept time to the preacher down the block. "One, two . . . three, four . . . one, two . . . three, four," until he got to fifteen, which was about how many souls were now raised from the depths of damnation over at the revival.

A bottle of Puerto Rican rum sat on an end table next to Richie. He not only dealt cards, but also served smooth glasses of 80 proof "Black Seal" on the rocks. With his left thumb wrapped around the neck of the bottle, he poured equal amounts for each player.

"Tilt your glass," he said.

Richie was married twice to the same woman. The first time they were divorced, the second time she ran off with their kid. He never talked much about those years. Richie never talked much about anything except boxing.

His passion was southpaws and his idol was Sugar Ray Robinson. The middleweight could go from both sides, but was a natural lefty.

Richie was fond of saying, "Whom the gods wish to destroy they call promising." He'd say that Robinson defied the rule; he had all the promise and all the reward.

This particular Saturday, the card game promised to be different and Richie knew it. A fourth player was sitting in. Richie was uneasy in his chair. He kept snapping the middle finger of his left hand in a low tone.

He turned to Eddie and said, "Where's your friend?"

"She'll be here soon," Eddie replied.

They were on their second hand and first glass of rum when the bell rang.

"I'll get it," Eddie said.

Richie reached for his glass and held it up to his lips. He peered over the top of the glass at the door, waiting for the fourth player.

When the door opened the preacher's voice poured into the room. "Alcohol is the devil's blood and gambling is the devil's down payment on your soul," he bellowed. "On your knees sinner, the wrath of God awaits you!"

Richie leaned forward in his chair and rested his left elbow on the table. Standing in the doorway, in between the devil's blood and down payment, was Eddie's friend.

"This is Sonja," Eddie said.

"Hello," Sonja replied.

The preacher was deep into the redemption of a soul as Sonja shut the door with her left hand. A duet of hellos answered Sonja as she turned back toward the table. Richie was still peering over the top of his glass as she made her way over to the card game.

Eddie began the introductions.

"This is Billy and Richie," Eddie said. "It's Richie's place."

"Nice place," Sonja said looking about the room.

"Like a drink?" Richie offered as he brought the glass down from his lips.

"Sure," Sonja answered.

Eddie took Sonja's coat and offered her a seat next to Billy.

"Thank you," she said as Richie reached across the table

lefty

with her drink in his left hand.

"Things are jumpin' next door," Sonja said. "There was a woman on her knees and a minister with his hand on her head."

"He's got a way with woman," Richie smiled. "I don't think he'd much care for our poker game; that is, until the fourth player arrived."

"Amen," Eddie said.

"Cut the cards?" Richie offered to Sonja.

She took the deck in her left hand and rolled half the deck over the other half without using her right hand or the table.

"Another lefty," Billy said.

Richie had known tonight's game would be different and now he knew why.

Sonja handed him the deck and he snapped the cards to the table. The preacher was right on time giving Richie the rhythm to deal a smooth hand. Eddie and Billy picked up the five cards with their right hands, while Richie and Sonja reached with their left hands.

Billy smiled as he fanned his cards out. Sonja and Richie showed no emotion while they spied their hands. Eddie was busy suckin' on an ice cube.

"I'll take two cards," Billy said.

Richie dealt him the two cards.

"Give me one," Sonja said.

"One?" Richie questioned.

"One," Sonja answered in a poker voice.

Richie slipped the card on the table. Sonja left it there. Richie lifted his glass and asked Eddie how many cards he wanted.

"Four," Eddie said as he placed the ace of diamonds on the table.

It was Richie's turn.

"I'll take two," Richie said.

He dealt himself the two cards. Sonja looked up from her cards and caught Richie's eyes. Neither one of them blinked. Sonja reached over and snatched up her card. Richie picked his two up and placed them with the other three. Eddie crunched hard on the ice cube in his mouth. Billy ran his left hand across his forehead.

"There ain't much happening in this hand for me," Eddie said over the sound of the crunching cube. "I'm out."

Billy spied his five cards. He reached down and slipped a five dollar bill on the table.

"Maybe I'm crazy, but I have good feeling with this hand," Billy said as he opened the bidding.

Sonja still had her eyes on her cards. The muffling sounds of the Pentecostal redemption filtered into the room. Richie had his right hand wrapped around the 80 proof. Sonja held her glass up. Richie poured a short refill.

"I'll see your five and raise you five," Sonja said.

"Your friends got a feeling for the game," Billy said to Eddie as he tossed his cards on the table. "I'm out."

Richie sat there with a lefty stare in his eyes. He had his mind on Sugar Ray Robinson. The hand had the all the promise and he was keen on reaping the reward. Robinson was a superior counter-puncher and Richie was going to have double up on his jab if he was going to win this hand.

"I'll see your ten and raise you ten," Richie said.

"Now we got a game going," Eddie injected as he leaned back in his chair.

"These two southpaws got that look in their eyes," Richie added like a ringside announcer.

This hand was a championship fight in the 15th and final round. Richie had countered with a Robinson-like combination of speed and agility. Eddie, Billy and Richie all had their eyes on Sonja. It was her move.

"I'll see your ten and call," Sonja said.

lefty

The speed of her counter to his counter caught Richie off guard. It was reminiscent of a Jake LaMotta chopping left hook. Richie could feel the canvas. He could taste the blood of a knockout blow. Sonja slipped her cards on the table. Three queens stared up at Richie and the other boys.

"Three queens," Sonja said.

"You're in trouble now," Eddie said to Richie with that half-smile people make when they're watching a fighter go down for the count.

"It's all yours," Richie said reaching for the rum.

Richie had been sitting on two pair, jacks high. It was a good hand and could beat most, but not this time. Sonja gathered up her winnings. A faint smile lit up Richie's face.

"Good hand," Richie offered to Sonja like a gladiator who could appreciate his conquerer.

"Thank you," Sonja answered.

Richie drew a mental picture of the hand. It was the first card game he had played with Sonja. He knew there would be more than a few hands in the future. But this was the first and it belonged to Sonja.

She caught his gaze. She could tell he was filling up the memory chip. She could sense the beginning of a thousand rematches.

"Your deal," Richie said handing the cards to Sonja.

The rest of the night was an even match. Even Eddie won a few hands. By 2 a.m. the tired eyes of a long night of card playing filled the table.

"That's all for me," Billy said as he held his hands above his head and stretched his back.

"Me too," Eddie agreed.

"That leaves you and me," Richie said.

"I'd better be going," Sonja said.

"I'll give you a lift," Eddie offered.

"No, that's okay," Sonja answered. "I live close by and

/93

could use the air."

"I'll walk with you," Richie said finishing his drink.

"Okay," Sonja said.

"Next Saturday?" Billy asked.

"Same time," Eddie answered. "You need a lift?"

"Sure, thanks," Billy said.

"Take care Sonja, I'll talk to you this week," Eddie said.

"Thanks for inviting me," Sonja said to Eddie.

"Thanks for not taking all my money," Billy joked.

"Good night," Richie said.

With all the pleasantries in the right place, Billy opened up the front door.

"It is never too late. Turn to Jesus now and you will be saved," came the calling from the preacher. Richie closed the door. He walked over to a chair and retrieved Sonja's coat.

"It's a little warm to be wearing a heavy coat," Richie said, feeling the weight of Sonja's garment.

"I always get a chill," Sonja said.

Richie draped the coat over Sonja's shoulders.

"Thank you," she said.

Richie acknowledged her thanking him by bowing his head. He reached for his keys sitting in a bowl on a bookcase by the door.

"Ready to go?" Richie asked.

"Okay," Sonja answered.

When Richie opened the door they were greeted by silence. There was no preacher preaching against the evils of life in the big city. There were no souls on their knees carving out pieces in the ground. There was nothing but silence and the flickering of an old streetlight in the 2 a.m. air.

"The preacher must have saved enough souls for tonight," Richie said.

"I keep thinking I need a little saving," Sonja said.

"Be careful," Richie said. "It might mess up your poker

game."

"Maybe you're right," Sonja said with a smile.

By now they had walked down the stoop and on to the sidewalk heading toward Sonja's house. As they neared the corner, they passed the Pentecostal church. It seemed closed and empty, except for one light that peered through the front door, which was still ajar.

"It's a beautiful church," Sonja said turning back to look at the building.

"It used to be a five and dime. When they turned it into a church the members spent a lot of time fixing the exterior and interior," Richie said.

The outside of the church was decorated with mosaic tiles. The colors were bright and could be seen in the flickering night of the streetlight.

"I've always wanted to see the inside of the church," Sonja said.

"Well, the door's open, so maybe we can peek inside."

"Okay."

Sonja and Richie made their way down the path to the open door. Sonja went first. Richie behind her. When she reached the door, Sonja hesitated.

"Maybe we shouldn't go in."

Richie stepped in front of Sonja and peeked through the empty door. He didn't see anybody.

"It looks empty."

Richie took Sonja's hand and led her through the door. The room was dimly lit. Sonja could make out the silhouette of folding chairs. They stood in neat rows of ten. Richie and Sonja walked down the center aisle toward the light.

Facing the rows of seats was an altar. It was simple. A huge velvet portrait of Jesus on the cross hung from a nail behind the a makeshift pulpit. The pulpit was an old wooden podium. One of its legs was missing. A couple of telephone books had been stuck underneath to keep it from wobbling.

The light came from a bulb hanging above the pulpit. It was no more than 60 watts. The dim light cast a shadow of some water pipes that hung from the ceiling across the velvet Jesus.

"Look at the velvet Jesus," Richie said.

Sonja walked up onto the altar. She ran her hand across the front of the podium.

"Jesus looks good in velvet," Sonja said.

Richie was up on the altar with Sonja. He stood next to her and leaned on the podium. His weight was too much for the old stand with the telephone book leg.

"Watch out," Sonja gasped.

It was too late. It went crashing forward. Richie went crashing with it.

"Ohh!" Richie yelped.

He hit the floor hard. The bible which was sitting on top went flying across the room.

"Are you okay?" Sonja said as she went rushing to Richie's side.

"Yeah," Richie said with a stunned look in his eyes.

"Let me help you up."

"I'm okay. Just give me a second."

Richie checked his body for broken parts. When he realized everything was in order, he started laughing.

"When I saw that bible flying through the air, I finally figured out what that preacher has been talking about," he said.

"It happen so fast. I got scared when I saw you lose your balance," Sonja said.

Sonja kneeled down next to Richie. She had her arm across his back. He was busy dusting himself off from the fall. It was at that moment that Sonja first noticed her. She was sitting on the floor in a corner of the room. She was a little girl wearing a white dress. Her hair was long and black. She had her knees curled up into her chest. She was staring at the light above the podium. Her eyes were fixed on the bulb.

"There's a little girl in the corner," Sonja said.

"What?" Richie asked.

"A little girl in the corner," Sonja repeated .

Richie turned around and caught site of the child. She was hidden in darkness. Her hair was luminous. Her gaze fixed on the bulb. Richie and Sonja got to their feet. He picked up the podium and set it back up on the telephone books. Richie reached across the floor for the bible. He clasped it in his left hand and placed it back on the podium.

Through all of this commotion the little girl did not move. She kept her eyes on the light.

"Do you think we should apologize?" Sonja asked.

"I'm not sure we should bother her. She seems deep in thought," Richie said.

"She's very beautiful. She looks mesmerized," Sonja said.

"She's my daughter," came a strange, yet, familiar voice from across the room.

"Her name is Millie."

It was the preacher.

"Welcome to our church," he said. "I've seen the two of you before, haven't I?

"We, I mean I, live next door," Richie answered.

"That's right. I knew I'd seen you," the preacher said.

"I'm just visiting," Sonja said.

"Good to meet both of you."

"And you," Richie replied.

"Is your daughter okay?" Sonja asked.

"She's fine," the preacher said. "She lives in her little world. "

"She's very beautiful," Sonja said.

"Thank you," the preacher answered. "She looks like her mother."

"She must be very beautiful, too," Sonja added.

"Her mother died a few years ago in a fire. Millie was in the apartment. A fireman got to her before the smoke. Her mother wasn't as lucky," the preacher said in a calm steady voice. "Millie hasn't said a word since that day. She just stares up at the sky or at a light. It is as if she sees her mother."

"I'm sorry," Sonja said.

Sonja walked over and ran her hand through Millie's hair. Richie looked back at the light. Millie sat there with her luminous hair staring at the bulb, her mother, never far from her side.

mAngO SHOeS

cleopatra on the delaware

There were sixteen entrances to the Maxwell House Coffee plant and all of them were shut. The time clocks ran out of time on April 14, 1992. The last 446 people who freeze-dried "America's favorite instant coffee since 1967" were out of a job by four thirty p.m. that Friday afternoon.

Counting himself one of the most unfortunate on that day was Bill Halloran. Bill had worked for Maxwell House for over thirty years. Marilyn, his wife, used to work in the plant's cafeteria serving piping hot coffee in the morning and soggy tuna fish sandwiches in the afternoon. She left the factory in 1976 and opened up Marilyn's Beauty Parlor, catering to the wives of the coffee workers. At Marilyn's you could get a new hairdo, a cup of her famous coffee and the latest gossip about life over at the plant.

Bill's son Chris started working for Maxwell House in 1979. Chris never had much ambition. He figured he'd follow his father into the factory and work his way up the line. He married Renee right after he got the job at the plant. They moved into their own railroad flat that same year. The seven rooms, with two windows in the back kitchen and two windows in the front bedroom, cost them 190 dollars a month. Renee worked part time at the concession stand in St. Mary's Hospital to help meet the rent. Money was tight, but life was good.

Chris started out as a pourer on the freeze-dried line. His position on the line was above two huge vats. Brewed coffee came pouring from overhead into the stainless steel containers. The temperature inside the vats was well below freezing. The brewed coffee was crystallized by evaporating the water with blasts of frozen air, leaving nothing but granules of coffee. The end product was instant coffee, a favorite in seven out of ten American homes.

Chris stood above the vats and below the pouring coffee to make sure there was no overflow and to regulate the temperature inside the vats. He wore a blue pinstriped uniform, a paper hat and waterproof shoes. He went through at least three uniforms a week because the coffee would pour over the sides of the vat and splash all over him.

He changed his shoes at least twice a day. After working three years at this position on the line, his toenails had taken on a permanent shade of brown, dyed by the fresh brew seeping between his toes. Chris used to joke that he never needed a cup of coffee in the morning—his toes provided him with enough caffeine!

Chris and his father ate lunch in the cafeteria each afternoon. Usually, they brought their own sandwiches. Prices on the lunch line had risen over the years while the soggy tuna fish had become even less appetizing. Bill Halloran still had a cup of coffee with his lunch; Chris preferred a soft drink.

In the spring of 1988 rumors started spreading about the closing of the plant. General Foods, the parent company to Maxwell House, asked employees to fill out questionnaires about working conditions, benefits, and years spent with the plant. One question that stood out for many workers was whether they would be willing to relocate.

Maxwell House had a plant in Jacksonville, Florida, that performed many of the same functions as the Hoboken plant, whose workers used to laugh about whether or not their Floridian counterparts all had blue hair and sun spots. Chris and his father never paid much mind to the questionnaire.

The Hoboken plant had over 1000 workers and had been producing coffee since 1939. Rumors about the plant closing had come and gone during all those years. This rumor was just like all the rest. People were drinking more coffee than ever before. Renee and Chris had their only child later that year. Bill Jr. weighed in at eight pounds, six ounces. He was a big kid, but that didn't matter to Renee; she was happy his toes weren't brown.

Bill and Marilyn were proud grandparents. Word of Marilyn's grandson spread at the beauty parlor. The wives of coffee workers showed up with presents on the days they were scheduled for new perms. At the plant, Chris and Bill handed out cigars at lunchtime.

Chris moved up from pourer to packer. Coffee jars ran single file down a conveyor belt. The granulated coffee poured into the jars through funnels. It was all synchronized to prevent any spillage. Chris stood at his station at the far end of the conveyor belt making sure that the vacuum-packed lids closed correctly on each jar. There was little mess and Chris was able to wear one uniform all week.

In 1991, Bill marked his 30th anniversary of working for Maxwell House. That same year the world around him began to change. Every other Friday was pay day. Checks were handed out over at the credit union after work. Each department had its own line. The queues were short and the reward was sweet.

But Friday, April 12th, 1991, was different. After putting in his eight hours, Chris went to get his check. Mrs. Carlton was the woman behind the cashier's window at the credit union. She'd been handing Chris checks for over ten years. This time the envelope was thicker.

He tore it open and slipped out the letter inside. It was from management and the news wasn't good. It read:
> Employee-
> Due to cutbacks, the plant will be closing
> in the spring of 1992. Additional information
> will be forthcoming. We regret this decision,

however, it was deemed necessary for the survival of Maxwell House.
Sincerely,
Fred Button

Fred Button was the Director of Public Information at the local plant. He always had a way with words—short and sweet. Chris read the letter over and over. There was a silence in the room. Heads were bent over, reading the note. Collective shock filled the credit union. Some workers received compensation packages. A few were offered jobs at the Florida plant. The majority were left to file for unemployment.

Chris was scared. He and Renee had a three year old son. An unemployment check for $240 a week was not going to cover the family expenses. Chris and Bill lasted at the plant until the final day. They watched as hundreds of workers were let go with little compensation and less hope. Bill Halloran missed out on retirement by three years. Over 30 plus years of working at the plant were about to come an end.

On the final day of operation, management held a coffee and cake party for the last of the workers. Men and women stood in their blue pinstriped uniforms, filled with years of coffee grime. They stood there eating coffee cake as the turbine engines that had helped to give the northeast its daily caffeine fix went silent.

The huge neon coffee cup on the river's edge did not light up that evening. After 50 years, the Maxwell House plant was gone.

Marilyn's Beauty Parlor closed within six months. Few wives had the spare money for getting their hair done. Marilyn said it was all for the best since she would have more time to spend with Bill.

The Seven Seas, a rough and tumble bar that was a favorite hang-out for plant workers, tried every kind of gimmick to stay open. It was a sports bar, a 50's revival bar, it even changed its name to O'Leary's hoping that an Irish pub might keep a crowd around. It was all to no avail. O'Leary's Seven Seas went the way of Marilyn's by the year's end.

Bill was without work for over a year. His unemployment was running out when he got the bright idea to take cooking lessons from Marilyn. He landed a job at a lazy hotel in New York City as a line cook. His job was to put the bacon on club sandwiches and cut them into four sections.

His pay was less than half of what he had made at the plant, but it was a job. Each night he brought home some leftovers for Marilyn. Her favorite was the pecan pie, made with fresh Georgia pecans. They'd sit in front of the TV each night eating leftovers and watching Jeopardy.

Marilyn always had the right answers. Bill encouraged her to try out for the show; it was money they could use. Marilyn said if she could play the game from home she'd think about it, but there was no way she was going on national television.

"Bill, you know how nervous I got even at PTA meetings," she said. "Can you imagine how I'd feel with Alex Trebeck standing right in front of me? Noooo way."

Chris spent almost two years looking for work. During those years his world fell apart. No work led to no money for rent. After the unemployment ran out, Chris and Renee couldn't meet their bills. They moved in with Bill and Marilyn for a time. Five people in a six-room tenement. Bill Jr. shared the front room with his parents.

Chris and Renee started fighting. Within two months, Renee had taken Bill Jr. and moved to South Jersey. She moved in with her cousin Jackie, and got a job on the boardwalk in Asbury Park. Jackie watched the boy while she was at work. Renee sold Berklee's Salt Water Taffy outside the only ride left on the old dilapidated boardwalk.

On Wednesday nights she worked at the Mayflower Bingo

Hall. She was a natural at calling out numbers:
> "These are the big games and the big prizes.
> Five in a line bingo . . . we play for the choice of the store, the very next game, the big game and thebig prizes . . . five in a line bingo, five cards for a dollar . . . "

Senior citizens from three of the local retirement communities took chartered buses every week to the bingo hall. They all agreed that Renee had a way with numbers and was the best caller at the Mayflower.

Chris moved in with his friend, Carl, who used to work at the plant too. Carl had gotten a job working for Frito Lay as a warehouse manager. In the summer of 1993, he helped Chris land a job as a delivery truck driver.

Chris' route took him through Newark, where he delivered to bodegas and candy stores. He carried a manifest to help keep track of the deliveries, the Weekly News, and a thermos filled with ice coffee.

He picked the truck up each morning in Jersey City at seven a.m. Another guy helped load him with potato chips (barbecue, sour cream, and onion), cheese puffs and tortilla chips. He usually slipped a bag of tortillas into the front seat to eat throughout the day.

It took Chris twenty minutes to get to Newark with the truck. His ride took him over the Pulaski Skyway. The road stretched above Jersey City and ended up in Newark. The bridge was named after the Polish, Revolutionary War general who helped the colonists defeat the British.

The summer of '93 was turning out to be the hottest in memory. The temperature reached over 100 degrees for 15 days straight in July. On July 16th the heat was overwhelming. By eight a.m. the temperature was 105 degrees. Warnings were being broadcast over the radio for people to stay indoors. Two guys from WBRM in New York were frying eggs on the steps outside the station.

As he made his way to Newark that morning, Chris listened to the radio and looked out the window at the landscape of gas tanks and burning dumps. On the Pulaski Skyway, he popped a tortilla chip in his mouth and put the truck in fourth gear.

Most of the traffic was heading in the other direction, toward New York City. Heat vapors were rising off the top of the cars stuck in the morning rush hour. A couple of overheated cars were pulled off on to the side of the road with their hoods up. Chris watched while one guy kicked the side of his Toyota.

"What you get for buyin' a foreign car," Chris said over the eggs cooking on the radio.

He pulled up to his first delivery on the north side of Newark right on time. Sweat was already pouring down his back. He had an extra t-shirt in the truck. He switched into it just before heading into Felix's bodega. He pulled out three trays of chips from the back of the truck to bring into the store. Cheese puffs and tortilla chips were the big sellers at Felix's.

"Hola, Felix," Chris said using the only Spanish he spoke.

"Buenos dias," Felix said moving over to the hold the door for Chris.

Chris put the trays down in front of the Frito Lay display and started putting the bags on the shelves. He had twenty Jumbo Cheese Puffs, thirty Salty Tortillas and twenty Barbecue.

The bill came to fifty dollars. Felix always paid in cash. He opened the register and pulled out five ten dollar bills. The humidity made the bills stick together. Felix counted the bills a second time to make sure an extra ten wasn't stuck to the other five.

"Okay," Felix said as he handed the bills to Chris.

"Gracias," Chris answered, the only other word he knew

mAngO SHOeS

in Spanish. "I'll be back next week."

"Okay," Felix repeated.

Chris picked the tray up and headed out of the store. He opened the truck's back door and climbed up inside. It was a little cooler in the trailer. He put the tray back in its bin and pulled a bandanna from out of his back pocket to wipe his forehead. He could feel the heat cooking the top of the truck. Chris knew it was going to be a long day. It wasn't even nine a.m. and he was already feeling the heat.

He jumped into the front of the truck and grabbed the thermos. He poured a full cup and drank it. The taste of coffee reminded Chris of his days at the plant. It reminded him of Renee and Bill Jr. He started the truck and headed to his next delivery.

There were four more stops on the north side. Chris made the deliveries with time to spare. He pulled the truck over to the side of the road under a tree to get some shade. Chris flicked the radio on and tuned in WBGA, a Newark jazz station.

The disc jockey was featuring the music of Cassandra Wilson. Chris had never heard of her, but he liked her voice. He slipped back in his seat and put his feet up on the dashboard. He poured some more ice coffee and sat there watching the sun bake the brick row houses across the street.

A group of kids were playing in an open hydrant up the block. They were all barefoot and wearing cut-off shorts. One kid cupped his hands around the water pouring out of the hydrant to make a huge spray. The other kids ran across the spray, cooling off from the hot sun.

Cassandra Wilson finished a song. The disc jockey came on the air to give a weather report:

> "It is eleven-thirty a.m. and this is already the hottest day in Newark's history. It is 116 degrees and temperatures are expected to rise

this afternoon. Health officials are warning people to stay indoors. Elderly people are especially warned to avoid any exertion, which may cause heatstroke. The extreme heat is dangerous. Stay tuned to WBGA for updates on the hottest day in Newark's history."

The music of Cassandra Wilson came back on the air. Chris felt her voice in his forehead. It was 116 degrees outside and here he was sitting under a tree in a Frito Lay truck in Newark.

"How did I get here?" Chris said to himself.

Chris drank the rest of the iced coffee from the cup. He pulled the bandanna back out of his pocket and pressed it deep into his eyes. He sat there with his eyes closed while the music of Cassandra Wilson eased his tension.

At first he didn't hear the two kids banging on the side of the truck. When he opened his eyes, he saw them standing outside his window. They were two kids from up the block. They were soaking wet and kept their hands pressed against their chests.

"Yo! Frito Lay man - How about a bag of chips?" one of them said.

"Let me get some barbecues," the other one said.

"Water must feel good," Chris said.

"Yeah, my man, come on, let me get some chips," the kid repeated.

"I can't. If I give a bag to you then all those kids are going to want some," Chris said while pointing at the kids playing by the hydrant.

"Well, then how 'bout all your money?" another voice said.

The voice came from over Chris' right shoulder. Standing on the runner of the passenger side of the truck was a guy with a gun. He had it pointed through the open window at

Chris's head.

"Don't shoot," Chris yelled.

"I ain't gonna shoot as long you give me what you got in your pocket, Frito Lay man," the guy said.

Chris looked back over his left shoulder. The two kids were gone. He saw them back down at the end of the block spraying water at each other. He'd been set up. It was his fault. He never should have pulled over in a neighborhood he didn't know.

"Come on, now," the guy said. "Give me what you got."

The guy was cool. It was the hottest day in the history of Newark and this guy was cool. Chris was pouring sweat. He put his feet down from the dashboard and reached into his pocket.

"I'm watching you," the guy said.

Chris pulled out the money from his deliveries. Everybody on the north side paid him in cash.

"Count it," the guy said.

"There's 250 dollars here," Chris said. "I know 'cause I just collected it."

"That'll do," the guy said, with the gun still aimed at Chris' head. "Hand it over."

Chris reached over and gave the guy the money. His hand was trembling and he was sure he was about to get shot. The gunman reached in with his left hand and took the cash. He stuck it in his pocket, pulled the gun down to his side, and started laughing.

"What you doin' sittin' here like this?" the guy smirked. "You just askin' to get robbed. Get your ass out of here."

Chris started the truck. He stuck it into first gear and headed up the block. As he passed the hydrant, the water came pouring in through the passenger window. Chris got drenched. The water felt cool against his skin. Cassandra Wilson was on the radio singing her rendition of Peggy Lee's

Fever.

Chris looked down at the *Weekly News* sitting on the seat. The headline read "Cleopatra on the Delaware." Below the headline was a photograph of a woman riding on raft down the Delaware River. On her head she wore a skull cap and had beads braided into her hair. Chris glanced at the photograph as the truck sped down the block.

He kept driving until he got out near Newark Airport. He pulled into the parking lot of a Days Inn Motel. He was soaking wet. He kept looking over his shoulder to see if anyone had followed him from the scene of the crime. There was no one in sight.

Chris never had a gun pointed at him before. The thought of getting shot in a Frito Lay truck in Newark on the hottest day of the century made him laugh out loud. It was a laugh filled with fear. Chris picked up the *Weekly News* . A plane took off overhead. He turned the pages until he found the horoscope. Renee used to read him his fortune by the stars every morning. "I trust Jeanne more than I trust my own mother," she used to say.

Chris was an Aquarian. He scanned the page to find his fate.

It read:
> Things are a mess. It is hot and the future is nothing like it used to be. I know it is a little late, but as for travel plans, today was not the day to take a drive. Chris, yes, I'm talking to you directly. Get out of that truck and run like hell.

mAng0 SH0eS

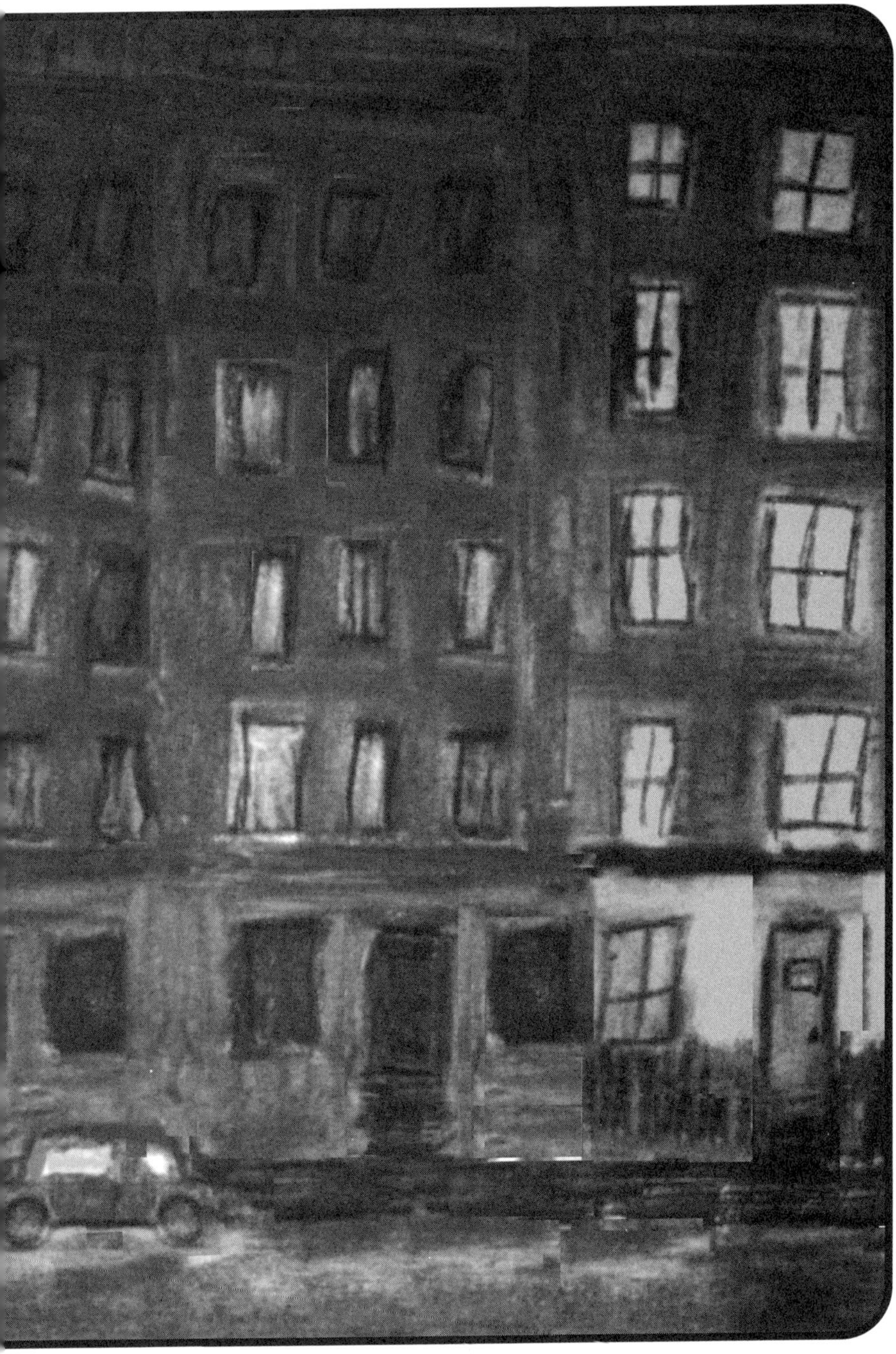

mAng0 SH0eS

pulse boy

Nine blocks from the Port Authority Terminal, seven blocks from the last place hell froze over, around the corner from where they held the 1994 Tony Awards, that's where Most lives.

It is 2 a.m. and I'm sitting in the Holland Bar staring out the window at two Brad/Tadd guys sniffing on the edge of some new rolled, nitrogen laced monkey-ass joint. The boys 2 men are standing in the same spot where I watched a guy who had no life lose his life on the streets of the grand city.

"See those guys," I said to the main man with the two-eyed mirror starin' him the face.

"They got the garment bag. You can't shake that no matter how many times you roll the monkey's end."

By now the Brad/Tadd guys had imbibed. The stretch marks that doubled for a limousine were moving in streaks along the sidewalk.

I've always been there for the short term. Never really had a home, just a little bit, maybe a little bit more, and then I'm on my way. Some people got friends to knock the day; me, I got attempts to knock my head off.

Late night suck downs at the Holland Bar, waiting for the one double-breasted mantra that died in the millennium grazing on the first and only triple decker dying machine. You follow? I'll lead you to the square, the almost definition inside the sexual encounter. Fuck me, Ingrid. I'm a pizza stone waitin' for the dough.

Come see Pulse Boy already scratchin' letters of disregard - the carbon copy, inflated doll with his hand down his throat. Can't find a good can of cream of corn anywhere these days. Anywhere these days- I've been there twice and

mAngO SHOeS

it's only on the second visit that you get to pull the chain that makes the monkey stand up and be noticed.

What is this shit about being noticed. The only notice I got was in the mail, and it ended up costin' me more than I had, cause I ain't got much.

They got circular stools for window seats at the Holland Bar. I sit in one waitin' for the bio-mass with the fine figure to swivel next to me. I'm sittin' here recalling a dream I had last night. Dream:

> Standin' sound dark on a meteor.
> My head is bent. I'm a meteor cow
> chewin' on the shot in the dark.
> I stick my nose down into the micro dust.
> I'm a dust cow searchin' for meteor
> truffles. Meteor truffles come poppin' out
> of the barren surface like the pope
> on a pizza stone. Wup! Wup! Wup!

"Wake up, Pulse Boy. You're wuppin' like the ole' dishwasher we had when we lived on Delancy Street. I thought maybe you were gonna drop an O-Ring and start spinnin' out of control- headin' straight for Valley Forge. Headed straight for the wig top father of our country. No comin' back from the garment bag, no comin' back from the wig top."

"Shit, Most, thanks for savin' Pulse Boy. Thanks for drummin' a soft growl and bringin' me back here, where the almost taste better with a little paprika spread across the doo-wop, yum-yum could have been."

"Sure, honey, just my way of sniffin' out the gotcha. See you later Good Humor man."

Back at the Holland Bar- 3a.m. I got my eye on the juice bible thumpin' away in the same spot where the Brad/Tadd guys puffed, where the nobody became a nobody. Here she comes. No Shit! The bio-mass in D minor with the fine figure headed for the swivel.

Fuck! The canary just died. The Welsh miner just

/116

dropped another quarter in the meter so he wouldn't get towed.

There she is sittin' in the swivel, fillin' up the space, blockin' the view of the juice bible, cuttin' out the paper men crunchin' hard on the 9th Avenue cracker jack.

"Hey honey. How's my meteor cow?"

"Moo . . . mooove over. Tell the monkey to sit down."

"I don't follow. Don't mean much unless you figurin' on sparin' me the juke box C-23 you been layin' on me all night.

    People all over the world join in
    on the love train, the love train . . .

Damn! The D minor slipped pass the terminal and headed over to 34th Street to catch the Pennsylvania 6-5000 over to love land.

Cross the river and there you got it. 36,000 wig top convertibles drinkin' down the shooter and firin' the cannon that burns off the calories. Another night in love land. A chance to run your hand through the big hair, to drive out the maybes, to wave good-bye to the Pulse Boy waitin' for the 63 that turned into the 126. Across the river rides the D minor to grandmother's house, checkin' if the coast is clear, cause the Pulse Boy ain't never comin' back.

"Honey, press C-22 for me."

"Sure, Most."

"I got the Tom Jones thing waitin' for the pizza stone."

    It's not unusual to be in love with anyone . . .

"Great Caesar's Ghost! I thought maybe Perry White might catch the 3:05 and join us."

"Fuck Perry White! He ain't nothin' but an Andy Rooney look-a-like."

"Look-a-like you been pullin' the chain a little much."

"Yeah, maybe you're right."

"Let's just stroll by the last place hell froze over and give up the swivel for another time."

"Okay."

It's not unusual to see me cry. I wanna die.

Back out on the street, I stomp, just in time to catch the last cracker jack. Just in time to be where I've never been.

"Hey, Most. I've been watchin' out for the Goo-Boy, standin' guard for the Dogwalker. Ain't nobody gonna put sprinkles on this side of the river."

"Good thing I got you off the swivel."

"Kiss me with that Export-A. Cover me up with that 300° blanket. Infusium, Infinitum."

Across the five lanes, beyond the exit ramp, skip a rock along 9th Avenue toward the flickering lights of love land.

"I ain't never goin' back, Most."

"I know Pulse Boy. I saw the monkey stand up. I gave the locksmith the key. He changed the cylinder. There ain't no back to go to."

So, here I am and here I stay on 9th Avenue where the Irish freckles blend in with the gum stuck on the sidewalk. Where the nic' of time can get a razor cut. Where the Pulse Boy can ride the Sweet Love until the moon drops.

"Come on, Pulse Boy. We got places to go and things to see."

"Okay, just gotta kick the can into the gutter one last time."

"Okay, Pulse Boy, but make it fast, cause the already is about to turn into the almost and sure enough don't wait for anybody."

"I got you Sweet Love. Draw the curtain. Pull the shade. As long as we got 9th Avenue, we got the horse and buggy, and that's sure enough for me."